THE

By

Riano D. McFarland

Vanity Inc.

Copyright © 2020 by Riano D. McFarland.

All rights reserved. No part of this book may be reproduced or transmitted in any form or by any means, electronic or mechanical, including photocopying, recording, or by an information storage and retrieval system, without permission in writing from the copyright owner.

This is a work of fiction. names, characters, places, and incidents either are the product of the author's imagination or are used fictitiously, and any resemblance to any actual person, living or dead, events, or locales is entirely coincidental.

Any figures depicted in stock imagery are models, and such images are being used for illustrative purposes only.

This book is dedicated to my brother, Huene D. McFarland, who inspired me to look beyond my perceived limitations as an author and explore the unfamiliar in the creation of my stories. His encouragement motivated me to think outside the walls of convention and envision things on a much grander scale.

Although his departure from this world came too soon, his memory and influence will live on forever within the pages of THE ARTIFACT.

Rest in peace, Big Brother.

CHAPTER 1

It had been careening through space for over a billion years. What began as a massive planetoid with a diameter of nearly six-hundred miles, had been whittled down from millions of years of intergalactic travel, colliding with other planetoids, being pounded by meteor showers, crashing through asteroid belts and space debris, slingshotting around planets, and fracturing against the atmospheres of countless celestial bodies before settling in on its final trajectory... Earth.

Trailing a few million years behind the asteroid which caused an extinction-level event that ended the age of the dinosaur, it entered Earth's upper atmosphere as a meteor the size of a large melon, shedding mass in the atmospheric burn-off before plunging into the frozen heart of a glacier at the edge of the arctic circle. After burrowing its way deep into the embrace of the surrounding ice, the red-hot meteorite was barely the size of an olive when it finally cooled and came to rest.

As ice ages came and went, the extra- terrestrial fragment was further compressed beneath the weight of millennia of snow, ice, and permafrost as the polar ice cap expanded and receded, pushing the fragment further south with each subsequent advance.

By the time the ice from the Pleistocene Epoch began to recede, the fragment had traveled as far south as the Great Lakes Basin where it was deposited along with six-quadrillion gallons of glacial meltwater and a variety of colorful stones scraped from the bedrock as the glacier plowed ceaselessly forward. On the pebbly shore of Lake Huron, it was in no way exceptional, actually paling in comparison to the smooth, brightly colored stones surrounding it.

It was oddly plain and misshapen with its only outstanding attribute being its weight which was easily five times that of other stones measuring twice its size. The dull bluish-grey color made it nearly invisible on a beach otherwise littered with vibrantly pigmented natural masterpieces.

Lying there in peaceful serenity, it remained undisturbed for another fifteen-thousand years as the stones surrounding it were collected by indigenous beachcombers and fashioned into Native-American jewelry and adornments. A Shaman from the Wyandotte Nation originally discovered the fragment, sensing the enormous energy radiating from within the heavy, bland object. He kept it, revering it as a magical totem and passing it down from generation to generation as the Wyandotte Nation enjoyed centuries of peace and prosperity.

By the mid-1600s, while the object remained within the tribe's possession, the reverence for it did not. After their Shaman traded the sacred object for two kegs of rum during a drunken stupor, turmoil erupted among the different factions of the confederacy. Not all of the tribes were receptive to the religion force-fed to them by the European "Blackrobes" and the resulting internal discord tore at the very fabric of their unified nation. Without the influential energy of the artifact, the Wyandotte Confederacy was decimated by tribal infighting, European-borne diseases, and attacks by adversarial tribes seeking to gain control of the vast territories formerly dominated by them.

The artifact itself, landed in possession of a British explorer by the name of Captain Garvey, seeking passage into the southern regions of the North American continent. His meeting with the Shaman was a customary show of respect, with each leader trading something of value signifying the validity of their accord. The two kegs of rum Garvey offered for passage were a lop-sided trade in the young Shaman's opinion. In order to avoid disfavor with the spirit world, he offered the explorer the deer-skin pouch around his neck containing the artifact, telling him "This will protect you during your journey."

Having more faith in their muskets and gunpowder than the rock inside a deer scrotum hanging from his neck, Garvey graciously accepted the talisman; however, deeming it non-essential, he left it in a locked chest at the garrison when he and his exploration party departed the next morning. Five days into their expedition, they were attacked and killed by Iroquois warriors.

The artifact remained undisturbed at the garrison along with the explorer's personal belongings for another two years before being collected by his wife, Elizabeth. With a modest inheritance from her father in Europe and the money her husband had saved to finance his expedition, she re-settled in Norfolk Virginia where she assumed management of the failing trading post her husband had boarded up years earlier in search of greener pastures.

Within days of her arrival, she was approached by plantation owners hoping to use the shuttered trading post as a hub for tobacco sales. Happy even to have been offered such an opportunity, she graciously accepted and within a few months, the trading post had become one of the keystone businesses in the entire Virginia Colony.

As the demand for tobacco grew, so did Elizabeth Garvey's wealth and status among colonial plantation owners. Being a focal point of the tobacco industry, she was confronted with the inability of tobacco plantations to meet the growing demands of worldwide export clients. At the start of the boom, plantations relied on indentured servants who worked free of charge to pay off their passage fees from Europe. With the continuation of the profitable tobacco market, those indentured servants were able to work off their contracted servitude obligations and were given land which allowed them to accumulate wealth and pay the passage fees to bring their family members over from Europe.

While the Virginia Colony had become the wealthiest and most populated British colony in North America, the falling numbers of indenturees directly impacted the ability of plantation owners to meet the growing demands for their product. In order to fill the labor void and ensure the continued profitability of their tobacco, plantation owners shifted their labor force from indentured servitude to outright slavery.

Unable to stomach the cruelty of selling human beings as if they were livestock, Elizabeth Garvey opted to retire, selling the business, and returning to England as a widow of great wealth and social stature. The chest containing the artifact and other belongings of her late husband was left behind; forgotten after years of storage in the dusty attic of the trading post.

Ownership of the trading post changed hands many times over the next century with each subsequent owner being able to build wealth even in times of war and unrest. However, in December 1775 while renovating the facility to include a second floor for additional living space, the new owner discovered the dust-covered chest still stored in the rafters. After breaking open the lock and emptying out the contents, he was disappointed to find there was apparently nothing of value inside the chest. Tossing it out onto the trash pile behind the store, he continued his renovations without wasting a second thought on the chest or its contents.

Later that day, one of the slaves tasked with stacking the rubble and burning it, noticed the pouch on the ground near the chest. Without a thought, he picked it up and slipped it into his pocket before continuing the task at hand. That night after retiring to the slave quarters on the outskirts of the city, he pulled the pouch from his pocket and opened it, dumping the artifact onto the straw mattress in front of him. As he reached out and took it into his hand, he felt a jolt of energy which instantly knocked him back onto the cold dirt floor of the dilapidated wooden shack. In his mind, he could see the entire journey the artifact had undergone on its way to that moment in which he clutched it tightly in his hand.

Placing the artifact back inside the pouch, he tied the ends of the deerskin straps into a knot and slipped the necklace over his head, concealing it beneath his dirty shirt before lying down on the lumpy bed. He was asleep within seconds. In the early morning hours of January 1st, 1776, as he slept, the British bombardment of Norfolk began, completely destroying the trading post and everything surrounding it. The young slave was oblivious to the attack as he continued sleeping peacefully through the night.

Upon awakening that morning, large areas of Norfolk were burning as British soldiers marched through the city setting the homes and businesses of revolutionaries on fire. Without fear, the slave walked up to the British soldiers and surrendered. Days later, he was enlisted into Lord Dunmore's Ethiopian Regiment.

During five years of fighting for his freedom under the British flag, he was never wounded or captured, and was one of only a few soldiers from the Ethiopian Regiment who was not infected by the deadly smallpox virus. In fact, by the time his regiment made it to New York, he was one of only a handful of soldiers who were still in good health despite the challenging conditions they'd faced. Due to his apparent immunity to the smallpox virus and overall good health, he was appropriated by Major Dunbar, a British physician, in order to assist in caring for wounded and infected soldiers.

While posted in the regional hospital in New York, the slave worked closely with Major Dunbar, and despite the deplorable conditions and barbaric methods used in caring for the sick and wounded, every patient the slave assisted the physician in caring for, survived. In many cases, they even recovered enough to be sent into battle again. Having never been given a name by his former master, the physician began calling him Lazarus due to the number of patients he'd helped bring back from the brink of death.

After the treaty of Paris was signed in 1783, Lazarus accompanied Major Dunbar back to England where he continued serving as his assistant for another forty years while, initially residing in the servant quarters of the physicians sprawling estate. During that time, he also received a modest salary which he diligently saved.

Within a few years, he'd mastered Oxford English and was present at every medical seminar attended by the physician. Due to Major Dunbar's failing eyesight, he took detailed, illustrated notes for the physician detailing medical advancements in anatomy, pharmaceuticals, and surgical treatments. By then, Lazarus had been the actual caregiver treating patients in Major Dunbar's office for many years.

In 1793, Lazarus asked for, and was given permission to marry Major Dunbar's housekeeper, Oleta. She was a stately, educated woman originally from the West Indies, and their attraction to one another was mutual and immediate. Even so, they kept the affair a secret for nearly a decade before being married. Once their union was official, Major Dunbar gave them the deed to a small parcel of land on the outskirts of London as a wedding gift.

With a portion of their combined savings, they built and furnished a modest two-story home while Lazarus continued working for Major Dunbar. Shortly before the birth of their first child, Oleta retired as the physician's housekeeper in order to provide full-time care for their family.

In 1823, the physician died, leaving his practice "temporarily" in the hands of Lazarus until another physician could be hired to take over the practice... Something which never happened for the remainder of Lazarus's life. Lazarus continued caring for patients and attending medical seminars even in the absence of Major Dunbar, taking and keeping detailed notes which, he willingly shared with other physicians practicing in London. Although he was never formally admitted to medical school, his detailed notes were required reading among medical professionals throughout Great Britain.

In the sixty-plus years he spent working as Major Dunbar's physician's assistant, Lazarus had gained the undiluted respect of London's medical community. His children, Thomas, William, and Elizabeth were all admitted to private institutions of higher learning, achieving academic credentials unheard of among people of African heritage in nineteenth century London.

Shortly before his death, Lazarus called his eldest son to his bedside. There, he passed the artifact on to Thomas advising him to keep it concealed on his person at all times and revealing that he'd been wearing it since December 31st, 1775 and had never taken it off. Thomas promised he'd do as his father had asked, accepting the heavy object, and placing it around his neck, concealing it beneath his shirt.

Later that same night, Lazarus died peacefully in his sleep on the evening of his one-hundredth birthday. One year after his passing, the Lazarus notes and illustrations were incorporated into an anatomical atlas by Henry Gray and Henry Vandyke Carter, which was then published in London in 1858. It would eventually become the enduring standard for anatomical studies in countries all over the world.

CHAPTER 2

While the origin of the artifact's energy would forever remain shrouded in mystery, it's presence on Earth was not. The young Shaman who foolishly gave away something which most certainly would have altered the entire course of Native American society, realized his folly upon awakening from his drunken sleep. The gravity of his actions left him little choice, but to try and retrieve it.

It took him and his party of scouts and warriors five days to catch up with Captain Garvey's exploration team. In attempting to cover up the loss of the artifact, he solicited the assistance of the Iroquois tribe under the guise of building a common defense against the pale-skinned explorers invading their southern territories. Claiming Captain Garvey had stolen his talisman after poisoning him with rum, he asked only that it be returned to him, leaving the remainder of the goods plundered to the Iroquois.

Without the protection of the artifact, he was unwilling to participate in the attack, but watched from a distant ridge while the Iroquois drew down on the exploration team. From the beginning it was a horrendous bloodbath.

Captain Garvey's men were all soldiers, quite willing to, and capable of defending themselves against aggression. The Iroquois warriors were also highly skilled and deadly fighters, employing techniques of attack previously unseen by European soldiers. As they collided in a barrage of musket fire, hails of arrows, steel sabers and tomahawks, the carnage was violent and shocking.

Iroquois warriors expecting an easy seizure of the exploration party's goods, were just as shocked as Captain

Garvey's men who expected the warriors to flee at the sight and sound of their fire-breathing muskets. In truth, it was a gory battle down to the last man standing, when the Iroquois scout chief killed and scalped Captain Garvey before bleeding to death from the musket ball buried inside his intestines.

After the bloody battle ended, the Shaman slowly rode down from the ridge into the now-silent pasture, oblivious to the acrid stench of gunpowder and death still lingering in the air. Even before dismounting his painted pony, he realized the entire battle had been an exercise in futility. The artifact wasn't there.

Walking past the mutilated and dismembered corpses of honorable men, both native and immigrant, the Shaman knelt in the blood-soaked dust beside the body of Captain Garvey. Rolling him onto his back, he verified what he already knew. The pouch was no longer around Captain Garvey's neck. Despite his inability to sense the artifact, he thoroughly searched each wagon, hoping he'd somehow recover that which he instinctively knew was not there.

It took the Shaman two days to dig the graves and bury the fallen warriors... of both sides. Afterwards, he collected their supplies and personal belongings and stacked them together in the center of the circled wagons of the expedition team. After releasing the horses which had survived the battle, he set fire to everything and performed an hours-long ritualistic ceremony asking the great spirits to accept each of the fallen warriors into their afterlives with honor.

Exiling himself, he remained in the uncharted wilderness of the southern regions for another two years. By the time he returned to the Huron settlement, most of his tribe had been decimated by rival Seneca and Mohawk warriors and scattered into the four winds. Those who remained were all but enslaved and living at the mercy of the European settlers.

As he approached the Garrison, he felt it... The unmistakable energy of the artifact. While it was faint, the Shaman could clearly sense that it had only recently been removed. Realizing it would be impossible to find anyone who could actually tell him when it was taken or who might have taken it, he could certainly ask around about recent arrivals or departures from the garrison.

Being that the garrison was more of a military resupply station than an actual community, there were arrivals and departures several times each month. Most were known traders and furriers who frequently traveled the trade route between the once-thriving Wyandotte territory and the Virginia colonies. Due to increasing tensions among the tribes of the Wyandotte Confederacy and instability of the relationship between colonial Europeans and the Native-Americans, traffic along the trade route had dwindled to a fraction of its former volume.

The departure of Elizabeth Garvey in the accompaniment of regimental soldiers stood out like a lighthouse in the mind of the Shaman. They'd been underway for only ten days when he arrived back at the settlement. While it was clear he could never intercept them before they reached the Virginia territories, he was certain he could detect the artifact's energy once in the vicinity of its aura.

The volatile nature of the trade route made it necessary to travel in numbers; however, any large group of warriors would likely be seen as a threat to colonial travelers. While travelers were apprehensive when it came to groups of native warriors, they almost never traveled the route without guides who were both familiar with the terrain and could speak the language of the tribes in order to negotiate with them should it become necessary.

It took nearly a month for the Shaman to be hired as a guide along with another scout for a relatively small party traveling to Norfolk. They were three days into their journey before the travelers invited their guides to join them for a drink. While the Shaman's resolve was solid, so was the temptation of the rum. Even the gravity of his prior actions which had undoubtedly altered the course of history as it related to the Wyandotte confederacy, weren't enough to give him pause before succumbing to the temptation of the fiery spirit.

As the travelers regaled one another with their exploits of bravery and heroism, the stories became more and more embellished until it would appear that the Shaman was travelling the route to Norfolk with a band of invincible warriors capable of defeating a hoard of murderous adversaries with their bare hands. After escalating their recollections to the level of absolute absurdity, one of the self-proclaimed demigods turned to face the Shaman, asking "So, Chief... What's your story?"

By this time, it was all the Shaman could do not to pull out his knife and gut this band of obvious liars; however, with great difficulty, he resisted the urge to do so.

Prodding the Shaman even further, the traveler asked, "How many White men have you killed?"

"None yet," replied the Shaman, slowly sipping rum from the tin coffee cup in his hands.

As the travelers fell silent, exchanging quizzical glances among themselves while trying to mentally interpret the Shaman's statement, he began telling the story of the artifact. He explained how it was originally discovered by a shaman high priest over a thousand years prior and passed down generation to generation until it came into his possession ten summers ago. Although he spoke softly, his words had a powerful effect on the band of men sitting around the campfire with him. In particular, the Iroquois brave traveling with them showed keen interest in the story, listening carefully to each and every detail.

The Shaman told of the artifact's power to shape destiny to the advantage of the one in possession of it, and how its influence had made the Wyandotte Confederacy indominable for centuries. As he continued, the warmth of the rum eroded his judgement causing him to reveal details of the artifact, the pouch in which it was carried, and the idiotic trade he'd made with Captain Garvey... A trade which led to the dissolution of the Wyandotte Confederacy in fewer than two years.

"What ever happened to Captain Garvey and his exploration team?" asked one of the travelers, recalling the high hopes and expectations among the Virginia colonies as they departed for the southern region. "After their departure, no one ever heard hide nor hair from them again."

"They were attacked and killed by Iroquois warriors a few days after leaving the garrison," answered the Shaman.

"This is bullshit!" exclaimed one of the drunken travelers, looking around at the group of men surrounding him. "Captain Garvey and his men, with or without a magic rock around his neck, were skilled soldiers and a damn ferocious group of fighters!"

"The Iroquois were also ferocious," stated the Shaman flatly. "The battle was violent and bloody. Captain Garvey was one of the last to die," he concluded, staring blankly beyond the fire which was slowly burning down.

The other Iroquois escort, while silently listening, knew most of the warriors who'd set out in search of Captain Garvey's expedition. Looking across the campfire into the glazed eyes of the Shaman, he suddenly realized why they had never returned.

"That's a damn lie!" shouted the traveler, clearly offended at the thought of Captain Garvey and his crew being slaughtered by a handful of ignorant savages. "Besides... wouldn't the stone have protected them from being attacked?"

"It was not with them," replied the Shaman. "I know. I checked all of the bodies, and everything loaded inside each of the wagons myself. He must have left it in the Garrison before departing on the Journey."

During the long silence that followed, the pieces began falling into place inside the minds of the eight drunken travelers. Without warning, one of the large men tossed his cup aside grabbing the knife sheathed on his belt. "You soulless son of a bitch!" he exclaimed as he leapt over the fire lunging at the Shaman.

Even with his mind clouded by the rum, the Shaman's reflexes were still razor sharp. He grabbed the man's outstretched arm pulling him off balance as he pivoted, removing the knife from his own belt, and pounding it into the spine of the lumbering attacker. The man was dead before he even hit the ground.

As the remaining men scrambled to their feet in an uncoordinated attempt to slay the Shaman, it quickly became obvious they were woefully outmatched. Ducking and weaving his way through the clumsy hoard of self-proclaimed champions, he dispatched them quickly as his knife found new blood with every slash, parry, and thrust.

Standing in the light of the fading campfire, he breathed heavily as his heart pounded inside his chest. The bodies scattered haphazardly around the campfire lay motionless as the dusty ground absorbed their essences while they bled out. Looking about at the fallen travelers, he was stunned by the strong forearm encircling his neck from behind while a sharp Iroquois blade was slammed into his chest. The other Iroquois guide held the blade firmly in place as the Shaman's body began to slacken against him.

As he slowly lowered the Shaman onto the ground and knelt beside him, the warrior said "You have disgraced our people and betrayed your sacred oath as a shaman. This death is better than you deserve."

The Shaman did not resist. Grabbing onto the arm of his fellow warrior, he said "You must not forget. You must never forget. Find the artifact and return our people to greatness."

"I am no shaman," replied the man. "I am a warrior."

"The artifact does not care," said the Shaman between gasps as the life oozed from his body onto the ground. "Find the person or place of the most prosperity in Norfolk, and there you will also find the artifact."

As the light faded from his eyes, the Shaman said "I was foolish. Now you must be wise. Tell our people the story of the artifact..."

Before he could complete the thought, he was gone.

Withdrawing his knife from the Shaman's chest, he looked around the camp, erasing any evidence of his presence in the travel party and disappeared silently into the forest surrounding them. It would only be a day or two before the scene of this massacre was discovered. By then, he planned to be as far away from it as possible.

During his intentionally circuitous route back into the Wyandotte territories, he vowed to share his knowledge of the artifact with the remnants of his people. Unknowingly, he became the founder of the first and most dedicated secret society in North America. A nameless society which would persist until the artifact was once again in the possession of the Wyandotte Confederacy... however long that might take.

CHAPTER 3

While the artifact was transformational in the lives of anyone in possession of it, not everyone was able to sense its influential energy. Even those who *did* possess it weren't necessarily aware of the object's power. After a while they would become complacent, attributing the fortunes afforded them by the artifact to their own spiritual, physical, emotional, and intellectual prowess.

As the Shaman explained while dying in the arms of the Iroquois warrior, the artifact does not care. It has no conscience which guides its power to shape destiny to the owner's advantage, nor does it differentiate between good and evil.

During the artifact's centuries within the Wyandotte Confederacy, it passed through the hands of many spiritual guides and leaders. While the entire confederacy benefitted greatly from its mere presence, the individual wielding it dictated the flow and purpose of that sphere of influence. While traits like honor and integrity were expected of a shaman from the Wyandotte Confederacy, who went to great lengths when examining the ethical qualifications for a successor, European settlers found the traditions and rituals of the Native American tribes senseless and overtly superstitious.

Just as confusing to the indigenous population was the religion of the "Blackrobes", who worshipped a single God that reigned over everyone and everything. Furthermore, their fervor in forcing that religion into the fabric of the Wyandotte Confederacy was met with staunch resistance among the various tribes, who felt their beliefs and traditions were being ridiculed and marginalized.

As one shaman explained it, "The rain cares not upon who it falls. The wind cares not which branches it sways. The sun cares not whose face it warms, and the seasons come and go without regard to the arrogance of men." Accordingly, the thought that a single deity could be supreme ruler over all of these things, seemed preposterous to them.

While the artifact inside the dust-covered chest of Captain Garvey's belongings had silently guarded its surrounding environments for decades, no one suspected it as the origin of their good fortune. Although the legend of the artifact was widely circulated throughout the remnants of the Wyandotte Confederacy, there were very few warriors left in any position to actually seek it out and recover it. With the fragmentation of the once powerful coalition, tribal infighting made it difficult for them to unite behind this, or any other joint cause. Although during the century that followed, the tribes would once again coalesce, leadership of the Confederacy would change hands between those tribes many times.

In the face of the obstacles presented, membership in the secret society dwindled; however, their crusade to recover the artifact persisted. The artifact's approximate location in Norfolk did not remain a secret for long. In fact, it was isolated within a year of Elizabeth Garvey's re-opening of the trading post but knowing where it was and retrieving it were two completely separate challenges.

The nature of the artifact is to protect and bend destiny to favor the person who possesses it... not a person who merely *seeks* to possess it. While there had been several attempts to locate the artifact and remove it from the premises, each attempt was thwarted by often unimaginable external occurrences.

One young warrior had watched the trading post for weeks, carefully observing the ebb and flow of customers and vendors who frequented the establishment. He knew precisely which window of opportunity could most easily be exploited to allow him undetected access to, and regress from the building, and enough time to locate and remove the artifact once inside. He'd shared his plan with other members of the secret society in case his attempt was unsuccessful and created several contingency plans to deal with obstacles which could arise unexpectedly.

He'd waited for a rainy, moonless night which would restrict visibility and provide him the cover of darkness while discouraging others from venturing outside their homes due to the adverse weather conditions. There was not a soul outside on the streets of Norfolk as the young warrior tossed aside the deer skin covering the foxhole in which he'd been hiding. Like a ghost, he darted across the slick, muddy street, approaching the ten-foot high wooden outer barrier surrounding the compound. Using his hunting knife and tomahawk he quickly scaled it without a sound. As he threw his leg over the top of the wall, the artifact intervened.

The jagged bolt of rogue lightning crackled violently through the night sky finding its mark atop the fence. In an instant, the once strapping young warrior was reduced to a charred shell, smoldering in defiance of the raging tempest seeking to extinguish his burning body.

While the resulting thunderclap physically shook the foundations of every building in Norfolk, leaving residents hiding under beds and tables or cowering in closets, there was only one fatality and not a single structure in the entire township was damaged.

By morning, the storm had passed leaving fresh air and clear skies in its wake, upon which to paint the new day. Arriving shortly before dawn, Mrs. Garvey's carriage driver unlocked and pushed open the heavy wooden gate before returning to the driver's seat and driving into the compound. The revolting stench of burning flesh was there to greet them as they rode into the compound.

To the right of the entry gate, the grotesquely charred shell of the young warrior dangled oddly from the high wooden wall. His left leg was wedged at the ankle between the tapered tops of the rounded logs which formed the barrier and was arguably the only feature of the disfigured corpse which could clearly be identified as human.

Later that morning, after dislodging and lowering it to the ground, the body was identified as that of a young Iroquois warrior named Dekanawida. While he'd been burned beyond recognition, both his knife and tomahawk were unique and unmistakable.

More confusing was the motivation behind his presence atop the wall. During the night of the incident, there was nothing inside the trading post worth braving such austere weather conditions in order to steal. The tobacco harvest from the regional plantation owners had been sold and loaded into the cargo holds of British naval vessels which were already well underway back across the Atlantic. As speculation surrounding the incident left colonists scratching their heads, the members of the secret society monitoring the artifact remained silent, blending inconspicuously into the background while never losing track of its location.

Even as the trading post changed ownership over the years that followed, the protection afforded by the artifact transferred seamlessly to the new owners even though they knew absolutely nothing of its existence there in the rafters of the aging building. Never forgetting the fate which had befallen the warrior, Dekanawida, none of the dedicated watchers dared attempt to remove the object by force or deception, understanding the consequences and futility of such actions.

After a century of unwavering dedication to silently monitoring the artifact, they were finally presented with an opening which afforded them the narrowest of opportunities in recovering it. The new owner of the trading post was renovating the facility and discarding everything left behind by the previous owners. When the trunk of Captain Garvey's belongings was finally tossed out onto the trash heap to be burned, the young slave who discovered and pocketed the artifact did not go unnoticed.

Within an hour, several watchers of the artifact were notified and hastily conceived a to plan to seize the pouch. Many of the Iroquois and Mohawk tribe members viewed slaves as the soulless property of the European plantation owners. While they had no grounds upon which to base that assumption, it was an opportunity unlike any other presented during the past hundred years and they were determined not to let it slip by without at least *trying* to exploit it.

Later that evening, one of the warriors secretly followed the young slave to his dilapidated quarters on the outskirts of Norfolk. The remainder of the hastily assembled recovery party waited in the forest near the trading post under cover of darkness for the scout to return with the location of the artifact. When he arrived, they quickly developed their plan of attack, hoping to execute a quick extraction and escape into the dark forest undetected.

As they were about to embark on their mission, the British ships in Norfolk Harbor began shelling the town with heated shot and hollow shells containing live coals. Being a centerpiece of commerce and trade in Norfolk, the trading post was the very first structure targeted.

Lord Dunmore's opening volley completely obliterated the eastern wall of the compound... The very same wall where the Iroquois watchmen had gathered to launch their raid and recover the artifact. In an instant, the secret society's numbers were cut in half with only a single warrior surviving the blast.

Gravely injured, he managed to escape into the forest avoiding the British soldiers who'd been sent ashore to sack the city and burn it to the ground. Outside Norfolk at the pre-determined rendezvous point, he mounted his horse with great difficulty and rode back to the region of the Huron tribes. A few days after sharing his story with the remaining members of the secret Wyandotte society, he died of injuries sustained during the blast in Norfolk.

CHAPTER 4

Once again, the artifact had demonstrated its power to shape destiny and protect anyone in possession of it. One might believe this would have been a clear deterrent to anyone seeking to rip it from the hands of its current owner.

It was not. In fact, the wild-eyed explanation of events as described by the dying brave were a catalyst, adding fuel to the fire already burning hot inside the hearts of the secret society members. As a result, their numbers doubled... but their tactics changed.

Instead of attempting to wrest possession of the artifact from its owner, the secret society would now employ a strategy of long-term patience and opportunistic positioning. While they renewed their vows to recover it and return the Wyandotte Confederacy to its former greatness, they also acknowledged the futility of attempting to steal it or take possession of it by force.

In order to acquire the artifact, it would have to be given freely by the person holding it. Therefore, members of the society would seek to remain in close proximity to it assuming an opportunity to gain possession of it would eventually present itself. They would employ any means necessary to be the recipient of the artifact when it inevitably changed hands and would even entice or cajole its present owner into joining their secret society voluntarily.

During the war for independence of the American colonies, Wyandotte secret society members closely monitored the young slave who'd surrendered to British forces the day Norfolk was set ablaze. They watched and waited in obscurity as he enlisted in Lord Dunmore's Ethiopian regiment to fight for his freedom. They witnessed the unlimited power of the artifact as other soldiers fell around him, mutilated and dismembered by colonial musket balls and canon fire. They watched as his entire regiment was consumed by the smallpox virus, leaving only him unaffected while his fellow soldiers withered away in agonizing horror.

Secret society members remained close and their resolve was further cemented when the slave began assisting Major Dunbar in the field hospital. The manner in which he could facilitate the recovery of even mortally wounded soldiers was undeniable proof that the artifact could even ward off impending death.

When Major Dunbar was released from military service in the American colonies and asked Lazarus to accompany him back to London, members of the Wyandotte secret society scrambled to find both a warrior who would follow the artifact, and a way to get him aboard the vessel bound for England. In the few days that remained before the ship would set sail, it would be impossible to arrange the logistics necessary in order to accomplish this last-minute feat.

However, as fate would have it, there would be a blood descendant of Powhatan, chief of the neighboring Algonquian-speaking tribe, who would most certainly not be refused passage to England aboard the Royal Navy's ship. It was none other than the great-great-grand-daughter of Rebecca Rolfe, otherwise known as Pocahontas.

While most descendants of Pocahontas opted to "pass" presenting themselves as White Anglo-Saxon Protestants, Mary Ann Davies was proud of her Native American heritage, choosing to gain as much knowledge of her ancestry as she possibly could. In pursuit of that knowledge, she traveled to the Virginia colonies to research and re-connect with her ancestors, embracing their heritage and traditions.

While the Wyandotte and Powhatan confederacies were not allied per se, whispers of the secret society and their crusade to recover the artifact were circulated among the tribes of both coalitions. Although members of the Wyandotte secret society were hesitant in doing so, they reasoned it might be their only means of remaining in close proximity to the artifact and reached out to approach Mary Ann Davies mere hours before she was to board the ship bound for England.

After being sworn to secrecy, she was reluctantly brought into the fold of watchers and enlisted to track the artifacts movements while in England. While she'd never imagined inheriting such an all-encompassing responsibility for the Native American Nation, she was determined to shoulder that responsibility with dignity and honor.

Aboard the ship during the voyage to England, she closely monitored the movements of Major Dunbar and Lazarus; however, at no time did she ever attempt to initiate contact with them. Nevertheless, she was acutely aware of the air of good fortune surrounding both of them. It wasn't that there were obvious occurrences which could be unequivocally attributed to the artifact, but rather a subtle tendency for things to work out in their favor, and in a broader sense, to the benefit of everyone else aboard the ship.

A prime example of that, was the weather during the voyage across the Atlantic. In the height of storm season, the ship didn't encounter a single day of rough seas. The weather, which was notoriously unpredictable during Atlantic crossings in August and September, seemed to either dissipate as the ship approached or move away from it so as not to affect the seas through which it must sail.

In expectation of the dangerous storms during the crossing, only a handful of travelers were willing to risk embarking on the journey at that time of year, and many of the scheduled passengers simply didn't show up on the departure date. As a result, every passenger aboard the ship was given individual quarters, including Lazarus. Furthermore, the ship's galley had stocked provisions for the crew and a full complement of passengers based on a voyage of sixty to one-hundred days. Instead, the vessel reached the British port in only forty-nine days, and while deaths were commonplace on such journeys, not a single person fell ill or died during the crossing.

Upon his arrival in London, Major Dunbar was able to re-establish his medical practice almost immediately. His seemingly magic touch when it came to the ability to heal any ailments or injuries, led to the rapid expansion of his patient list, and earned him a stellar reputation among hospitals and medical professionals across England.

Mary Ann Davies, through her discreet surveillance of Lazarus and Major Dunbar, was able to document the plethora of unusual and miraculous occurrences surrounding the Doctor and his brilliant medical assistant. After decades of observation, her attitude and appreciation for them evolved as she surmised the artifact had probably chosen Lazarus who, even realizing the power it afforded him, never sought to exploit that power, or use it to the detriment of others.

Even after getting married and having children, she continued her passive surveillance of Lazarus and throughout his childhood, encouraged her son, John, to embrace his ancestry and their traditions. Eventually, she divulged the existence of the secret society and passed the responsibility of observation on to him.

While John Davies and Thomas Dunbar were of approximately the same age, the dedication each of them displayed regarding their heritage was worlds apart. While John willingly assumed the mantle of responsibility passed on to him by his mother, Thomas soon grew tired of wearing the heavy object around his neck. The object which had shaped destiny and allowed him to lead a life of privilege, now seemed too cumbersome a burden for him to bear. He'd never known hunger or desperation or endured the shame of being owned by another human being and was therefore, skeptical as to the inherent benefit of the artifact his father had passed on to him. He attributed the unimaginable string of favorable circumstances to his own intense study habits, exemplary work ethics, and dogged determination to succeed.

Lethargy towards the artifact slowly took hold. At night, Thomas would remove the necklace before going to sleep, setting it on the nightstand next to his bed. He'd leave the house without it more and more frequently, and soon it simply became another object in the nightstand drawer, rarely ever seeing the light of day.

In keeping the promise to his mother, John Davies kept constant watch over Thomas Dunbar's activities in London. Enlisting in London's Metropolitan Police Department, he worked a district which allowed him to inconspicuously observe Thomas's daily routines. Eventually, he was promoted to a detective position, giving him unrestricted access to pertinent investigations in order to solve open cases and apprehend criminal offenders.

One late summer afternoon, John was called to the scene of a gruesome murder. In an apparent act of passion, a man had killed his wife and her lover after catching them in bed together. While the police had secured the scene and arrested the husband who willingly surrendered without resistance, the bodies weren't moved until Detective John Davies arrived at the hotel. His shock was palpable when he realized the dead Black man atop the equally dead White woman, was Thomas Dunbar!

Under the guise of searching for evidence, Detective Davies scoured the room looking for the pouch containing the artifact. His heart was pounding in his chest like a drum as he searched every corner of the hotel room including both bodies and their discarded clothing which littered the floor around the bed. Unable to find it there, he expanded his search to Thomas's house where he discovered the pouch containing the artifact buried at the bottom of the nightstand drawer.

His pulse was racing as he removed the deerskin pouch from the drawer. He was expecting to feel something... anything which would validate the power harbored within the heavy, but otherwise nondescript object. Loosening the straps at the top of the pouch, he cautiously dumped the artifact onto his bare hand. Still, other than the object's size-to-weight ratio, he felt absolutely nothing out of the ordinary.

Actually, taking possession of the artifact was disappointingly anti-climactic for someone who's ancestors had risked everything just to regain ownership of it. Slipping it into his pocket, he left the bedroom and exited the premises with the two police officers who'd been waiting outside the room.

Back at the police station, Detective Davies completed his written report and turned it in without mentioning the item he'd removed from Thomas Dunbar's bedroom. Since his childhood, he'd been living with the knowledge of the artifact and hearing tales of its supernatural powers. Now, clutching it in his hand inside the pocket of his overcoat, he felt oddly depressed. It was as if he'd reached the end of an amazing journey only to find the coveted prize had already been removed.

For days, he sluggishly moped around his apartment feeling as if the walls were slowly closing in on him but lacked the drive to venture outside for more than a few minutes. In the blink of an eye, he'd lost any sense of motivation for police work, and summarily resigned from the police force without explanation. After writing a personal letter for delivery to Achak, the shaman and secret society liaison between North America and the British Empire, John became a total recluse.

The letter gave detailed instructions as to his address and the location of the artifact inside his apartment. It was clear to him as he wrote it, that he wouldn't survive the six-month response period between him sending the letter and the arrival of the secret society's emissary to retrieve the artifact.

In essence, the artifact was doing exactly what it always did... bending destiny in favor of the person in possession of it. Unfortunately, from his early childhood, John Davies had been singularly focused on obtaining the artifact. He lived, breathed, and wished for nothing else, irreversibly tying his destiny to finding and securing the artifact. With that mission accomplished, his destiny had been fulfilled.

Three weeks after delivering the letter to the courier service, John Davies died peacefully as he slept.

CHAPTER 5

Two weeks passed before anyone missed him, and another before the stench of his rotting corpse became unbearable for the other residents in his building. By the time police officers entered the apartment, Detective Davies body was partially liquified and completely disgusting.

While his living space was somewhat disheveled from lack of attention, there were no obvious signs of forced entry or a struggle of any kind. The molding fruit and partially evaporated tea inside the cup on the end table beside him were apparently untouched, and there was absolutely nothing which pointed toward foul play. The chair in which he was seated faced the window looking down on the busy street below. His legs were crossed at the ankles and his arms were positioned on the armrests as if he'd been sleeping.

Regardless of the total lack of evidence suggesting his death was anything other than natural, any former police detective discovered dead inside his locked apartment would generate a certain degree of suspicion. However, even after a thorough examination of the remains, there was no indication that external factors played any role in his death. In fact, it appeared that Mr. Davies, for all intents and purposes, had simply stopped living.

Regardless of whether John Davies' death was a result of foul play or natural causes, in 1865, London was the world's most densely populated city, and apartment space there was at a premium. After the initial investigation concluded, the landlord was eager to renovate and prepare the apartment for new tenants as quickly as possible. Under normal conditions, he would have been very selective in screening applicants; however, the unexplained circumstances surrounding the death of the previous inhabitant presented a serious obstacle in finding new renters.

Even after thoroughly sanitizing the apartment, the light smell of death was still noticeable and acted as a powerful deterrent for nearly everyone who viewed the domicile. After nearly four months of vacancy, the landlord lowered the already discounted rental fee again and was finally able to find a new, although somewhat mysterious tenant.

The man was obviously a person of great financial means and was completely uninterested in viewing the apartment before renting it. Furthermore, he signed and paid for a full two-year lease in advance via a private courier who also took possession of the door keys for the new tenant. The name on the lease was Doctor Stephen Redding.

He moved into the apartment unseen by anyone else in the building and made no effort to make the acquaintance of any of the other tenants. While he could be heard moving heavy objects and arranging things inside the flat at times, for the most part he was a silent occupant who avoided any and all contact with his neighbors.

Two months after Doctor Redding occupied the apartment, Achak's emissary from the secret society arrived in London. upon debarking from the ship, he made his way directly to the address John Davies had indicated in his letter. Outside the door of the apartment as he stood there poised to knock, an intense sense of foreboding came over him. It was so negative, it actually prevented him from following through with the knock.

Backing away from the door, he became nauseous and ran down the stairs, vomiting in the gutter outside the building. Gazing upward at the window overlooking the street, he could clearly see the silhouette of a man observing him from the apartment. While he was unable to identify any details regarding the spectral figure in the window, of two things he was absolutely certain. First of all, the person watching him had most definitely discovered and taken possession of the artifact. Secondly... He was consumed by evil.

While most humans are in a constant battle with their better or worse angels, the person looking down on him had no such conflicts. He had completely acquiesced to the darkest elements of human nature. His malevolent energy was further amplified by the power of the artifact with which it had completely melded.

The young emissary was now facing an entirely different situation. While as a shaman, he was able to clearly sense the energy of the artifact, he was also acutely aware of his inability to retrieve it. Standing there in the rapidly darkening streets of London, he realized he was a at distinct disadvantage. Still, his commitment to the cause of the Wyandotte secret society was absolute.

While he had been given enough money to complete his mission and return to Norfolk with the artifact, this new development would require immediate adaptation. After checking into a nearby tavern under the name Wyatt Hawk, he immediately wrote a letter to Shaman Achak detailing the developments surrounding the artifact and explaining the need for a broader net of observation in a city the size of London. He also described the aura of evil enshrouding the person currently in possession of the artifact, and informed Achak of the need for the heightened spiritual fortitude among the members dispatched to London in order to assist in monitoring it.

For weeks, Wyatt Hawk covertly monitored everyone who came and went from the building, carefully documenting their arrival and departure times and, when possible, their destinations and actions taken while there. Within a few days, he knew more about each of the building's occupants than did any of the people who actually lived there. Still, the mysterious specter who possessed the artifact seemed never to leave his apartment. Two months into his stake-out, that changed.

During an intense rainstorm, he caught only a fleeting glimpse of a dark figure darting out of the building and quickly disappearing around the corner into the adjacent alley. Wyatt left the tavern seconds later, catching up to and stalking the stranger as he closely hugged the walls along the deserted alleyway.

For most people, following this target would have been virtually impossible. The man was tall and slender, wearing a black oilskin overcoat and wide-brimmed hat pulled down to shield his eyes and face from the wind-blown rain. His gait was long and purposeful as he quickly yet quietly covered ground, slipping in and out of shadows which rendered him nearly invisible. Despite his best efforts to conceal his movements through the abandoned streets and back-alleys of London, Wyatt Hawk was unshakeable.

As a child, Wyatt's father had taught him well and honed his skills as a tracker. By his tenth summer, he could track a wounded deer through thick underbrush in the dark of night until the animal collapsed from the arrow piercing its lungs. In his mind, he could still hear his father's voice saying, "Become the animal and flee as it would flee, escape to where it would escape, and hide where it would hide."

While the sprawling city of London was a world away from the shores of Lake Huron, his ability to track this human prey was just as keen as it had been with other animals. In addition, his ability to perceive the aura of the artifact was so strong, it was as clear to him as the beam of a lighthouse. Even in the driving rain angrily pelting the city, the glow surrounding his target was intense and unmistakable.

Under the eaves of a building two or three miles from his apartment, the stranger stopped. Looking over his right shoulder, he noticed what appeared to be a feral cat crouching beneath the stairs of a fish market loading dock. Pulling a small piece of meat from his coat pocket, he knelt and slowly extended his hand towards the apprehensive creature. The smell of the raw red meat was too enticing for the cat to resist, and he left his hideaway slowly approaching the stranger. As he cautiously extended his body to accept the unexpected treat, the stranger deftly slit the animals throat with a long, sharp knife!

It happened so quickly that the young shaman nearly missed it. From a safe distance, Wyatt Hawk observed as the stranger removed a sack from beneath his overcoat and stuffed the dying animal inside of it. While the rain washed the cat's blood into the gutter behind the fish market, the strange man made his way back down the alleyway right past the invisible young shaman who was one with the shadows.

Sticking to the shadowy recesses of the city, the oddly slender man hastily made his way back to the apartment building, and quietly slipped inside.

The actions of the stranger left Wyatt Hawk, quite frankly, perplexed. From his perspective, it seemed the man had purposely wandered the streets in search of a victim. The cat seemed to have simply been a target of opportunity which happened to be in the wrong place at the wrong time.

While following the man back to his apartment building, the young shaman seemed to feel the artifact's aura darken ever so slightly. Whenever he drew too near the stranger, the ominous sense of dread he felt physically turned his stomach and made it difficult for him to even breathe. At one point, he felt as if he would go into cardiac arrest if he didn't immediately evacuate the direct vicinity of the artifact.

Entering all of these details into his secret ledger, Wyatt Hawk took time to underscore this particular effect, highlighting it for anyone who would possibly assume the role of surveilling and observing the artifact in the future.

In the ensuing decades, there would be many "Wyatt Hawks" occupying that room in the tavern... each of them as reclusive as the object of their surveillance. The stranger possessing the artifact continued his random and infrequent outings, randomly killing small animals and house pets throughout London before returning home with his bloody bounty. His modus operandi, while unpredictable in frequency, was always consistent in its execution. In the late summer of 1888, it veered drastically off track in a horrifying new direction.

As the acting Wyatt Hawk followed the stranger through the foggy streets of London's East End, the lanky man stopped near the corner of a dark alleyway. Expecting to see him bag his domesticated prey for the night, the shaman's blood ran cold when a young prostitute approached the stranger, emerging from the darkness through the thick fog.

Prepared to abandon his oath of passive surveillance, the shaman drew his knife and ran towards her, attempting to intervene in what he knew was inevitable. Before he could reach the two silhouettes disappearing into the foggy alley, the dark energy of the artifact hammered him to his knees, nearly choking the life from him. He listened helplessly as the young woman screamed over and over again until the killer finally slit her throat silencing her permanently. Under the cover of darkness, he heard the stranger slashing the young woman's body over and over again.

With herculean effort, the shaman dragged himself away from the artifact and into the shadows where he could finally breathe again. After a single deep breath, he vomited forcefully emptying the contents of his stomach all over the garbage stacked haphazardly in the filthy alleyway.

By the time Wyatt Hawk's head was clear again, the stranger was gone. With the sound of police whistles approaching in the darkness, the shaman slipped into the shadows and made his way back to the tavern. Across the street, the aura of the artifact was bright and angry. At long last, the stranger seemed to have discovered the prey he felt was capable of stilling his blood lust. He could not have been more wrong.

After the first of his murderous outings on August 31st, 1888 the stranger began a spree of killings which continued into the latter part of November of that same year. While the citizens of London collectively held their breath as the bodies of four additional prostitutes were discovered, each one brutally murdered and disfigured nearly beyond recognition. Newspapers seemed to sensationalize one aspect of the killings, focusing narrowly on the prostitution angle of the murders. In their haste to sell papers, they'd completely ignored the missing orphans, homeless vagrants, and elderly citizens who'd gone missing, to say nothing of the scores of domesticated animals which had mysteriously disappeared over the years.

Wyatt Hawk did not. He documented everything in excruciating detail, realizing the authorities were no closer to apprehending this madman than they'd been after the very first murder attributed to him. In an effort to call attention to the murderer he'd been observing for over a year, he composed a letter which he delivered anonymously to the Central Office at Scotland Yard.

Unfortunately, his letter, along with hundreds of others submitted by frantic citizens, were either dismissed as lunacy or lost in the chaos as law enforcement professionals frantically searched to apprehend the killer. Suddenly it became clear to him, that if this killer were going to be stopped at all... it would have to be Wyatt Hawk who stopped him.

Explaining his revelation in a detailed letter to the aging shaman, Achak of the Wyandotte secret society, Wyatt Hawk requested another shaman be dispatched to London aboard the next possible vessel. In the week that followed, he fasted while spiritually cleansing his aura through prayer and ancient rituals passed down through generations of shaman leaders before him. Afterwards, he prepared a single arrow, coating the arrowhead with a deadly poisonous paste extracted from the fangs of venomous North American water moccasins.

Folding all of his clothing and placing his remaining belongings together neatly on the bed, he sat quietly near the window waiting.

Visibility was near zero when the stranger slipped out of the apartment building into the drizzling rain wearing the ominous black oilskin overcoat. In contrast, the shaman was nearly naked, wearing only a traditional loincloth. His body and face were decorated with war paint, and a quiver containing the single poisoned arrow was slung over his shoulder. In his left hand, he held the bow given to him by his father the evening before he departed for London.

As he stalked the murderous stranger through the city, he was aware of everything. The purification ritual had sharpened his senses to extreme clarity. It was as if he could see through the rain, fog, and darkness cloaking the city. For the past several months, he'd been stalking the artifact. Tonight, he was stalking a killer.

Following the tall, thin stranger through the dark city, Wyatt Hawk watched as he approached Blackfriars Bridge. At the halfway point, framed by the Saint Paul's Cathedral looming ominously in the background, the stranger suddenly stopped. First, looking back over his shoulder, he then turned to face the young shaman who had already notched his arrow and was aiming it the stranger in the middle of the bridge.

"I know why you're here." said the stranger. "You're looking for this." he added, removing the pouch containing the artifact from his left coat pocket and holding it up in front of him. In his right hand, he held a pistol.

"The only problem," he added "is that you can't take it from me, can you?"

"No," the young shaman replied. "You are wrong. Tonight, I am not here to take the artifact. I am here to kill you."

On the bridge, the stranger lifted his right hand aiming and firing just as Wyatt Hawk released the tainted arrow. Both the flights of the bullet and the arrow were true, unerringly finding their marks.

As the bullet slammed bluntly into the shaman's chest, he stumbled backwards before falling to his knees at the edge of the bridge. In the distance, he could see the arrow had penetrated the stranger's left shoulder just below his collarbone and was protruding from his back. His left arm dangled limply at his side and the pouch containing the artifact was lying on the bridge in front of him.

The aura around the artifact lightened immediately as the tall stranger turned on wobbly legs attempting to continue across the bridge. After only three or four steps, his body began shaking uncontrollably as he lost his balance, his eyesight, and his sense of orientation. Stumbling toward the edge of the bridge, he fell into and over the siderail which would most certainly have been a sufficient barrier to a person of shorter stature.

Looking up into the rain falling gently onto his face, the shaman closed his eyes and smiled as the life's blood drained from his body. In his mind, he was home again looking out across the pebbly shores of Lake Huron in the midst of his tribal ancestors who were blessed with abundance.

Below the bridge, the embodiment of evil was swallowed up completely by the polluted waters of the Thames river and swept out into the North Sea, never to be seen or heard from again.

CHAPTER 6

It was just lying there in his path as the young street urchin made his way across the bridge. Each day, he'd set out before sunrise so he could reach the plaza outside of Saint Paul's Cathedral before it was overrun by vagrants, thieves, pickpockets, and beggars.

Every morning, he would sweep the plaza clear of leaves and sticks, and remove the rubbish blown in or left there by visitors and costermongers the previous day. As compensation, he was paid a sixpence per week and fed a hearty breakfast of bacon, eggs, stale bread, and milk or weak beer before heading off to school near the cathedral.

At the age of nine, Christopher was the oldest of seven orphans living in a foster home across the river from Saint Paul's where he and three younger boys shared a small, over-crowded room. Other than a place to sleep sheltered away from the elements, the drafty house offered little in the way of creature comfort. Nevertheless, it was a place for him to store his meager belongings and enjoy a warm meal before bed each evening.

That particular morning as he made his way across the foggy bridge, the pouch there at his feet seemed to defy the attempts of the thick fog to obscure it from view. Although Christopher knew the way from the house to the cathedral by heart, the decreased visibility made it difficult for him to see any further than his own outstretched hand. In fact, he'd run right past the body of Wyatt Hawk without ever seeing him.

After looking around attempting to pierce the wall of fog surrounding him, he quickly reached down and picked up the pouch before continuing on his way toward the cathedral. While he immediately noticed the small pouch was unusually heavy, he stuffed it into his pocket without examining the contents, opting to open it only after reaching the safety of the cathedral.

The Dean met him at the plaza entrance with folded arms and a raggedy broom, informing him that he was a few minutes late and would need to make up that time.

"Yes, sir," replied Christopher, taking the broom, and immediately getting to work on sweeping the plaza. Just as he was finishing up the stairs, the Dean called him inside for breakfast. After washing his face and hands in the water bowl provided by the Dean, he took his seat at the table and ate breakfast with several other members of the cathedral staff.

As usual, everyone ate in silence individually contemplating the daily tasks ahead of them. Upon finishing his breakfast, he rinsed his plate and utensils and placed them in the dishrack to drain. Before scurrying out the door, the Dean pressed a coin into the boy's palm, reminding him to arrive early the following Monday.

All things considered Christopher was a truly fortunate young boy. While the industrial revolution brought prosperity to Britain, only a few years prior, children of his age worked dangerous jobs in coal mines or as chimneysweeps. After parliament passed the Factory Act of 1878, those jobs were eliminated for children under the age of ten, making it difficult for boys like Christopher to find work at all.

Christopher's mother died while giving birth to him and his father was killed five years later when the mineshaft where he worked collapsed, burying him alive along with five other workers. Even after losing both parents, he completely escaped the fate of many foundlings and orphans who ended up in workhouses thinly disguised as orphanages and was placed in a foster home run by Mother Potts.

Understandably, Mother Potts was a strict but compassionate woman. Unable to have children of her own, she'd been caring for homeless and abandoned kids for most of her adult life. She provided for their basic needs, preparing nourishing meals, mending their clothing, and recycling the garments among her foster children as they grew into and out of them, and ensuring each child had a place to lay their heads each night.

While Mother Potts received government stipends for each foster child in her care, she insisted that working children make household contributions based on their income. Christopher was happy to contribute a portion of his weekly salary in order to make things better for everyone living there and each week, would leave two pence on the small table in the kitchen where Mother Potts took her morning tea. Additionally, he placed three pence in a biscuit tin, which he also entrusted to her care.

In truth, Mother Potts never spent a penny of Christopher's money. Instead, she saved every cent in a mason jar which she kept hidden away in her room for him alongside his biscuit tin. After three years, he'd already accumulated a tidy sum which he would receive either when he was adopted, or when he was old enough to leave the home to live on his own.

Each Sunday morning, she and her gaggle of foster children would march in formation across the bridge to attend early mass at Saint Paul's Cathedral. It was on one such morning that Christopher noticed the clutter littering the grounds of the plaza and, unprompted, began picking it up... something which did not go unnoticed by the Dean.

Approaching Christopher, he said "Sunday is a day of rest, young man. On the seventh day, even God rested."

Sheepishly looking up at the Dean looming over him, Christopher said "I'm sorry, sir. I just wanted it to look nice for everyone coming to mass this morning."

"Well," said the Dean, smiling. "It does look much nicer now. How would you like to make a regular job of it? Monday through Saturday, of course," he added, handing Christopher a penny.

"That would be wonderful!" exclaimed Christopher.

"I'll pay you a penny per day and feed you a hearty breakfast before school," stated the Dean. "You can start tomorrow morning, and I'll pay you a sixpence every week on Saturday."

Without another word, the Dean turned and walked back into the sanctuary, leaving Christopher outside smiling down at the very first penny he'd ever earned. That had been nearly three years prior, and after that, Christopher never missed a day.

Having discovered the pouch on the bridge earlier that morning, Christopher sat there in the classroom, consciously aware of the heavy object tucked away inside his pocket and dying to take a peek at it. After school, he raced home and disappeared into his bedroom just before noon.

As a foster child sharing a room with three other boys, privacy wasn't something taken for granted. However, for those times which demanded a degree of discretion, the boys would use their top sheet to cover themselves as they sat in the middle of their beds. Upon seeing this, the other boys mutually agreed to respect the privacy of the covered individual without prying.

There beneath the sheet, Christopher carefully opened the pouch wondering what he'd found. All morning, he'd fantasized about giant gold nuggets, precious stones from the Queen's crown jewels, and rare Oriental jade figurines. Sitting there looking at the unremarkably ugly grey stone, he was understandably somewhat perplexed.

Removing the artifact from the pouch, he scrutinized it from every angle, assessing its size and weight while trying to imagine exactly where it might have come from. After what seemed to have been only a few minutes, he tossed aside the bedsheet to discover the sun had set hours earlier and all of his foster-siblings were already sound asleep! Tiptoeing toward the bedroom door, he opened it to find the entire house was dark and even Mother Potts had retired for the night.

Outside in the distance, Big Ben solved the mystery rattling around inside the young boy's mind. Four quarter bells followed by ten chimes. It was now ten O'clock in the evening!

Earlier that morning, he'd stopped only briefly to observe the pouch on the bridge before picking it up and continuing on to the cathedral. Even though he'd taken that same route every morning for the past three years, somehow, he'd arrived at the cathedral nearly fifteen minutes later than usual.

Mother Potts had left a covered plate of food for him on the countertop near the stove to keep it warm. Carrying it into the dining room, he placed it and the artifact on the table. While eating, he curiously eyed the pouch careful not to stare at it for too long.

The questions firing off in his mind came at the speed of light. Could this ugly grey stone actually change his perception of time? What happened to the people around him as he skipped ahead? Was this something he could control, or was the stone actually controlling him?

After cleaning his plate and utensils and putting them away, he returned to his room and climbed back into bed. This time, he slept.

CHAPTER 7

Promptly at 5:30 in the morning, Mother Potts roused Christopher with her gentle knock at the bedroom door. He awoke refreshed and energetic, quickly dressing and dashing toward the front door. Pausing at the kitchen, he peeked inside saying "Thank you for last night's dinner, Mother Potts. It was really delicious."

"You're very welcome, Christopher," she said, smiling to herself. "Now run along. You owe the dean fifteen minutes and he'll be expecting you to arrive earlier this morning."

"Yes, Mum," replied Christopher as he sprinted out the door. Beneath his shirt, the pouch containing the heavy artifact seemed as light as a feather.

He reached the cathedral just as Dean Richard William Church was coming out the side door of the sanctuary, broom in hand.

"You're even earlier than I expected," said Dean Church almost melodically as he realized Christopher was already there.

"Yes, sir," replied Christopher. "I'm sorry about Saturday morning. Somehow, I lost track of time on the way here, but I can assure you it won't happen again." Taking the broom, Christopher hurried off into the plaza to begin his daily chores.

At the door, Dean Church lingered for a moment turning to observe Christopher's obvious enthusiasm in clearing the plaza. He was a good boy and a very dependable worker.

Before hiring Christopher, Dean Church would personally sweep the steps and the landing directly below them each Sunday morning. His idea of the job was to sweep the clutter out into the plaza and let the wind carry it wherever it may. That

Sunday morning before Mother Potts arrived with the children, he had actually done just that.

Watching Christopher properly finish the job he'd only half-heartedly begun was eye-opening for the dean. He realized that like so many people, he'd simply been sweeping problems away from his doorstep without actually solving them. It was a revelation worth far more than a penny per day, taught to him by a six-year-old boy who'd never even held a penny before.

That simple revelation fundamentally changed Dean Church, revealing to him that the Church of England's responsibilities extended far beyond the steps of the building, deep into the surrounding community. From that point forward, he viewed the church as an extension of the community rather than treating the community as subordinate to the church.

This shift in thinking led to subtle changes which benefitted everyone while also elevating Saint Paul's status. As a result, the dean was able to make significant progress on the cathedral's restoration, increase cathedral revenues by expanding the congregation, and reorganize the cathedral staff to more accurately represent the needs of the community.

For Christopher, it was a penny per day and a warm breakfast for something he'd have happily done for free.

That morning, in addition to the bacon and eggs, there was cold milk and warm, freshly baked bread for breakfast. With his work done and his belly full he headed off to school vowing to test his theories regarding the artifact and its ability to influence time.

Christopher loved school. The learning process itself, was fascinating to him. One morning you go to school not knowing how to spell your name, and at the end of the day... you could. With or without the artifact, time passed quickly for him while immersed in the learning process and, as usual, the school day ended much too soon.

On the other hand, Christopher now had time to further investigate the unusual stone inside the pouch hanging around his neck. While London was a densely populated city, most of its residents gravitated toward places where they could associate with others. This left plenty of places along the Thames for a young boy to escape the turmoil and tumult of industrialized London. His favorite was a shaded area outside the plaza near the cathedral overlooking the river below.

He would often sit there for hours, remembering how his father would go there with him after mass on Sunday mornings. As a child, they were some of Christopher's very first memories and the location held a special place in his heart.

Finding a spot on the grassy hillside, he sat facing the river and pulled the pouch from beneath his shirt. Loosening the straps, he removed the heavy object and held it in his hands. The moment it touched his skin, he immediately noticed things around him visually accelerating. After dropping it back into the pouch, he discovered a barge he'd seen approaching the bridge from his right was already passing underneath it to his left. In only a few seconds, the barge had covered a distance which normally would have taken at least ten minutes.

That essentially meant his perception was moving slower than time, remaining in a moment beyond which time had already progressed. Considering that point, he wondered if the effect could also be reversed, allowing him to travel back in time. Closing his eyes and concentrating his thoughts on that outcome, he took the object into his bare hand once again. The result was astounding!

Everything around him slowed to an apparent stop! While he was obviously unable to step back beyond a point in time which had already passed, he was able to slow time's progression to a point where he could move about freely in a world where everything else was virtually paused.

For the remainder of the day, Christopher experimented with the artifact to discover the advantages, limits, and potential dangers associated with time manipulation. In fact, the object seemed to actively assist him in discovering its hidden potential. The more he handled it, the more tightly fused with it he became. By the end of the day, he no longer needed to hold it in his hand to tap into its energy. As long as the pouch was worn around his neck, he remained connected to it and could draw from its energy instantaneously.

In Christopher's mind he felt that, in a sense, the artifact was self-aware. While it had no means of physically transporting itself or manipulating other objects around it, it could, when necessary, bring external natural or supernatural factors into play in order to prevent involuntary changes in ownership.

Once bonded with a new owner, it could only be released by death, abandonment, or voluntary relinquishment by the person in possession of it. Aside from that, it seemed the artifact's mission was shaped solely by the person holding it.

While Christopher understood the potential benefits and dangers of time manipulation, he also realized that, should the power of the stone ever become public knowledge, thieves and scoundrels would employ any means necessary in trying to wrest it away from him. Therefore, he was careful not to use the artifact's energy too often or in obvious ways and took great measures not to change things which would dramatically affect those around him.

His use of the artifact was initially limited to small things like speeding through a laborious Sunday morning mass or slowing things a bit so he could finish his reading assignments in school. Even so, his actions did not go unnoticed for long.

One morning as he was sweeping the plaza outside the cathedral, Christopher saw a face he'd not seen before. While new faces in a city the size of London weren't an uncommon sight, this one belonged to a man who simply seemed out of place. In an instant, time slowed, and Christopher walked over to the man who'd been peering around the corner at him.

The man's skin was reddish-brown, and his long straight black hair was stacked atop his head disappearing neatly beneath a stovepipe top hat. On his wrist, he wore a leather bracelet adorned with beads fashioned from multi-colored polished stones. Following a thorough inspection of the man from head to toe, he returned to the plaza to finish his work before going inside for breakfast.

After breakfast, as Christopher hurried along to school, he caught another glimpse of the man following him at a distance. While he never felt in the least bit threatened by the elusive stalker, it was clear to him that he'd been drawn there by the energy emanating from the artifact.

Suddenly, Christopher realized the existence of the artifact was no longer his secret. At a minimum, one other person knew about it and where there was one, there were bound to be others.

Wyatt Hawk had arrived in London two months after his fellow shaman's body was discovered on the bridge. He moved into the tavern which was already leased under his name and paid through the end of the year.

"Welcome back, Mr. Hawk," said the landlord, handing him the key to the room. "I hope your travels were successful."

"Thank you," replied Wyatt Hawk, nodding as he accepted the key and made his way up the stairs to his room.

Inside the room, everything was exactly as his predecessor had described in his final letter to Shaman Achak. Underneath the floorboard at the northeast corner of the room, he discovered the journal which documented decades of observation conducted by Wyatt Hawk behind many different faces.

After a bit of local research, he was able to ascertain that Jack the Ripper's killing spree had abruptly come to an end. While Scotland Yard may not have solved the cases or apprehended the murderer, Wyatt Hawk knew why he'd suddenly vanished. His brother's aim had been true.

It took him a few days to locate the artifact; however, by monitoring the bridge where the unidentified Native American Indian's body was discovered, he soon detected its aura in the possession of a young boy. Since the boy's daily routine was absolutely predictable, it wasn't very long before Wyatt Hawk could monitor his actions, accurately predicting when, where, and how to track him.

While observing him in the cathedral plaza, he noticed something previously undetected by other watchers assigned to observe holders of the artifact. He vanished! It was only a momentary flash, but the shaman clearly saw him disappear at one point then reappear several feet away from the spot where he'd previously stood.

He also noticed how the boy could sit absolutely motionless for extended periods of time. The longest of these episodes was nearly two hours as he sat in a field overlooking the Thames. Amazingly, while engaged in these inanimate states, no one could approach him or even come within several yards of him. Afterwards, he would awaken from his trance-like interludes picking up exactly where he'd left off as if nothing had happened.

Legends told of the artifacts ability to bend time for the first few generations of shaman leaders; however, it was something which hadn't been witnessed or documented for hundreds of years. Wyatt Hawk was certain that the young boy had discovered how to unlock and utilize this ancient method of time manipulation, which made him incredibly powerful and potentially... extremely dangerous!

While the potential for evil exists in each of us, Christopher was a special young man. For a child, he was exceptionally benevolent and in the wake of his vanishing spells, something positive would invariably occur which otherwise might have ended in disaster.

On one occasion, a stone mason working atop the scaffolding erected around the cathedral tower, lost his footing. While reflexively reaching out to grab onto the scaffolding and stabilize himself, he dropped a heavy iron hammer he'd been using which then plummeted towards an elderly woman leaving the sanctuary, oblivious to the impending danger from above.

Although several people witnessed the event unfolding before their very eyes, none of them were close enough to intervene in what was certain to be a most tragic accident.

At the last possible instant as those with weaker constitutions averted their eyes in horror, the hammer suddenly changed its trajectory, miraculously crashing into the marble steps behind and to the right of the unsuspecting woman. The shattering stone sent shards of marble in every direction; however, none of them even slightly grazed the woman who'd just narrowly escaped tragedy.

The boy who'd been sweeping leaves at the outer edge of the plaza, vanished before suddenly reappearing just outside the gate of the courtyard. In the blink of an eye, he'd moved over one-hundred feet from his previous position, unnoticed by everyone with the exception of Wyatt Hawk.

The following Sunday, the sanctuary was filled to capacity, with others waiting outside in the courtyard and in the adjacent plaza as word spread of the "miracle" at Saint Paul's Cathedral. Within a month, the size of the congregation doubled and then doubled again over the ensuing three months.

While most of these benevolent occurrences were much more subtle, they continued to a lesser degree, following the boy as he grew into a young man.

By the turn of the century, Christopher's passion for education and propensity for saving nearly every cent he'd earned, resulted in his acceptance to the University of Birmingham with a full scholarship upon the recommendation of Dean Gregory at Saint Paul's Cathedral.

Diligently applying himself, Christopher absorbed knowledge like a sponge, and in 1910, he received his Doctorate degree in Education. Shortly thereafter, he was offered a permanent position abroad at the prestigious New York University in the United States of America.

After nearly 130 years abroad, the artifact and its watchers from the Wyandotte secret society were finally coming home.

CHAPTER 8

The technology and ships making the Atlantic crossing from England to the United States had made incredible progress since the artifact's voyage from New York to London. Five days after departing England aboard the RMS Lusitania, Christopher was on the deck staring across the railing at the Statue of Liberty... a moment which, despite his urge to prolong, he chose to absorb in real-time.

Reflecting on his personal history, he considered it remarkable that an orphan without a drop of royal heritage could find himself aboard a modern steam ship, about to embark on a journey as a professor teaching European history in America. While, admittedly, the artifact had allowed him to take advantage of how time elapsed, it was never the source of his ambition, and he'd never used its energy to the detriment of others.

Two years after joining the faculty of NYU, Christopher met the woman who could slow time around them without the aid of anything other than her sweet voice and soft brown eyes. Her name was Anna Price, and he knew from the moment she applied for the job as his professor's assistant, that their bond would evolve into something special. That "something" turned out to be a wedding, a son, and two beautiful daughters who were all the joy of his life.

Along with his family, his reputation as an educator grew over the years because he had a knack for finding creative ways to make historical facts come to life in the minds of his students. He would often remind them that they were living in historic times and that tomorrow's history was in the making today.

As the years passed in New York, the Wyandotte secret society continued their strategy of long-term patience and surveillance, always keeping track of Christopher without ever approaching him. In fact, most of the members had great respect for him and his conservative use of the artifact.

While he was fully aware of the fact that his actions regarding the artifact were under constant observation, he wasn't always sure who was monitoring him... nor did it matter. The watchers never intervened or interfered in his life or sought to influence the decisions he made. While they were apparently well-organized, and the faces surveilling him had changed many times over the years, he sensed that their intentions were ultimately honorable.

As he dug into his career as a college professor, he cherished both the opportunity to impart knowledge to future generations as well as the chances presented him to interact with other professors in a wide variety of educational fields. While his children had grown into adults, embarking on their own life's journeys, he discovered the bond shared between this gifted assembly of professional educators was every bit as durable as that of the society of watchers who'd been shadowing the artifact since his childhood.

The depth of knowledge within that inner circle, although fluid in nature, was truly awe inspiring. Surrounded by contemporaries such as Albert Einstein, Nickola Tesla, Edwin Hubble, Thomas Edison and a plethora of other progressive thinkers, Christopher was at home in their midst soaking up knowledge with rarely a comment.

The one rare exception was his disagreement with Mr. Einstein regarding his theory of time and time travel. While seated together at a café in New Jersey, Albert laid out his theory, proposing that all things existed at all times, and that the past, present and future were therefore, all connected. He further maintained that if a person were able to travel at an extremely high rate of speed, they could in effect, "outrun" time, navigating forwards and backwards along the invariable timeline in both directions infinitely at will. Christopher disagreed.

"Might I suggest an alternative theory, Mr. Einstein?" asked Christopher.

"The floor is yours, Professor Nolan," stated Albert, simulating a genuflection.

"Your theory is based on attaining a velocity approaching or exceeding the speed of light. According to the British astronomer James Bradley, the speed of light is approximately 295,000,000 meters per second," stated Christopher. "While I accept that science and technology may one day advance to a point where travel at lightspeed is possible, the energy required to reach such a velocity would be immense for anything larger and heavier than photons, which have a mass of zero."

"I submit," continued Christopher "that the more practical solution would be to maximize time utilization by slowing the rate at which it progresses while maintaining the individual ability to move at a normal, unaffected pace within that window of decelerated time progression."

Furrowing his bushy eyebrows, Mr. Einstein replied, "You're suggesting it would be easier to slow time's progression than it would be to increase the velocity of an object to match the speed of light?"

"Precisely," replied Christopher.

"If you can accomplish that, my friend, you will have solved the most perplexing puzzle for all of mankind," replied Mr. Einstein. "Time is linear. It is constant, and it is the most valuable asset anyone could ever hope to possess. The ability to manipulate it lies far beyond the capabilities of human beings," he added.

"As does currently the ability for us to travel at the speed of light," replied Christopher. "However, if we can fully utilize time as it progresses, the net result would be the slowing of it, effectively making more of it available, while neither adding to nor subtracting from it," he added.

"For instance," Christopher continued. "the monogramed handkerchief currently in your breast pocket is not already in the breast pocket of the man sitting over there near the window. However, by slowing the progression of time while continuing to move through it at an unaffected pace, one could manipulate objects and otherwise maximize time utilization, making it seem as if they had traveled into the future, when actually they'd only taken advantage of the perception differential."

"That seems a bit far-fetched to me, Professor Nolan," said Albert, shaking his head. However, looking down, he noticed the handkerchief which had been in his pocket mere seconds ago, was missing. Shocked, he looked across the café at the man sitting next to the window. There in his breast pocket was the monogramed handkerchief of Albert Einstein.

Standing and smiling, Christopher left the money for his tea and biscuit on the table before picking up his satchel. Politely nodding at an obviously dumbfounded Mr. Einstein, he said "It was wonderful chatting with you my friend. We'll see you next week."

After that day, the two of them never discussed the theory of time travel again; however, over the years that followed their friendship and respect for one another deepened and remained steadfast until Mr. Einstein's death in 1955.

While Christopher's career was never in the headline of any publications, his balanced method in imparting knowledge was something his students and fellow faculty members greatly appreciated and benefitted from during his tenure at New York University. Even in difficult times as humanity faced two world wars and a myriad of other social challenges, his ability to find time for each of his students seemed inexhaustible.

Using the artifact, Christopher was able to create that extra time and use it to the benefit of his students. Of course, there are consequences associated with temporal manipulation. While others slowed metabolically along with time as he skipped about, researching solutions inside a bubble of deceleration, he did not.

Each time he used the artifact, he aged ever so slightly while those around him did not. Even with the beneficial energy of the artifact protecting him, he'd aged more rapidly than he most likely would have under normal time progression.

In 1969, the ground seemed to fall out from under him when his wife Anna was diagnosed with lung cancer. Determined to find a cure after her physicians had all but given up, Christopher spent nearly a month in decelerated time attempting to find a treatment which could cure her. When he re-emerged, his attempt had been unsuccessful, and his life's energy was almost completely drained.

That very same night, he left their home and walked across the street to a diner he frequented after Anna's health began to fail. Inside, he walked down to the end of the counter, taking a seat next to the man sitting there silently with his cup of cold coffee.

"Mr. Hawk," he said softly, causing the man to turn and look at him. "I have something I'd like to give you."

Reaching behind his neck, he untied the straps of the deerskin pouch and lifted it from beneath his shirt. Taking the man's hand, he placed the pouch containing the artifact in it saying, "Use it wisely, my friend, and it will serve your people well."

"Thank you, Professor Nolan," said the stoic man with the utmost respect. "You are a great philanthropist and have earned the admiration of the Wyandotte people."

Nodding and patting the man on the shoulder, Christopher turned without speaking to walk back toward the exit. Before he reached the door, the man added. "May your final journey be a peaceful one... my friend."

Smiling and nodding again, he left the diner without looking back. The scent of Autumn was in the air as he walked slowly down the sidewalk towards New York University Medical Center. He felt unusually light without the artifact around his neck and smiled as he recalled the day when he'd discovered it there on the Blackfriars Bridge in London a lifetime ago.

Upon reaching the Hospital, he continued inside to Anna's room in the medical ward and sat in the chair beside her bed. She was sleeping soundly as he took her hand in his. After a few minutes, he joined her in her dreams as he drifted off to sleep beside her.

Neither of them would awaken again.

CHAPTER 9

That monumental moment in which Wyatt Hawk received the artifact on behalf of the Wyandotte secret society set a chain of unanticipated reactions into motion. While the Wyandotte secret society had been watching and attempting to recover the artifact for over three-hundred years, in that time the demographics of the society had changed.

As tribes were scattered and systematically eradicated by the European incursion into their former territories, the Wyandotte Confederacy, for all intents and purposes, had ceased to exist. What remained was a secret society bearing the Wyandotte name but consisting of members from tribes and confederacies scattered all across the North American continent.

In the absence of a clear leader for the fractured Native American population, the leader of the secret society became the de facto custodian of the artifact. While a wise and competent individual, Shaman Huene was no diplomat.

Where his predecessor, Shaman Achak had endeavored to remain connected to the numerous tribal leaders whose people constituted the very fabric of the Wyandotte secret society, Shaman Huene was at a distinct disadvantage, having never been a part of a functioning Native American confederacy. By nature, a secret society is cloaked in obscurity. Lacking a century of Shaman Achak's inherited verbal history, it was impossible for Huene to reestablish those contacts without divulging the existence of the artifact and the society sworn to recover and protect it.

While every member of the secret society knew Shaman Huene, they did not know anything about one another beyond their shared name... Wyatt Hawk. Furthermore, many of those members were lone wolves, having severed ties with their own tribes in pursuit of the Wyandotte secret society's centuries-long crusade to recover the artifact.

Once the object was voluntarily and unexpectedly returned to Wyatt Hawk in that Manhattan diner, true ownership of it was effectively undefined. Each member of the secret society, including Shaman Huene, had sworn an oath to return it to the Wyandotte Confederacy vowing never to take personal ownership of it.

Although the society members had done so, the artifact itself, had sworn no such oath. Nature deplores a vacuum, and the one left by the Wyandotte secret society in regard to the artifact was monolithic. An object which had completed a billion-year journey through a universe filled with obstacles in making its way to our planet, was certainly not intended to lay at rest in a lockbox buried in the bottom of a desk drawer.

Having gained possession of the artifact, the secret society had quickly become passé, and after a year of virtual imprisonment, the artifact wanted only one thing... out!

While the secret society's codename Wyatt Hawk was meant to keep the identities of its members confidential, it did draw the attention of various law enforcement agencies after protests by Native American nations erupted, demanding ancestral lands be returned to their tribes. The majority of those protests were peaceful in nature, but on a few of them, one name raised red flags... Wyatt Hawk.

The name had been reported in connection with suspicious activities in New York and New Jersey on numerous occasions since the 1960s. Believing a Native American uprising was imminent, heavy-handed federal agents raided the office of the Native American Historical Society, seizing all of their documents and materials including the lockbox in Shaman Huene's desk.

As a team of FBI agents poured through the evidence collected, the lockbox was discovered containing several passports under the name Wyatt Hawk, each with different photographs and birthdates. In the bottom of that box was the pouch containing the artifact.

Unsure what to make of it, it was sent to the Smithsonian Institute in Washington DC for further analysis. Surprisingly, carbon dating revealed that the pouch was nearly two-thousand years old; however, analysis of the artifact inside it was inconclusive. To be more specific, the heavy bland object was of undeterminable origin because it was impossible to gather even the most miniscule of samples from it.

Any attempts by researchers to scratch, cut, chip, burn, drill, melt, pulverize, or otherwise penetrate the surface of the object were met with absolute failure. It was also impervious to any form of radiation, and spectrographic testing left researchers similarly frustrated. In fact, scientists working together to analyze the artifact would often be overcome by fits of rage resulting in actual physical altercations between them.

In short, the artifact repelled every attempt to define its chemical composition or to determine its point of origin, while apparently turning those analyzing it against each other. After a month of escalating tensions within the team without any notable progress in determining what it was or where it came from, the artifact was transferred from the Smithsonian Institute to the Pentagon.

There in a subterranean vault inside the country's most secretive organization, safeguards were put in place to limit the exposure time of each person working with the curious object. The artifact was once again subjected to rigorous testing, yet it refused to yield even a single clue as to its origin or chemical composition. It was also impervious to all forms of irradiation, remaining neutral when other objects and substances instantly became radioactive.

Another highly unusual characteristic of the artifact discovered by military physicists was its aversion to high altitude. The object could actually alter the gravitational field surrounding it, making it physically heavier as the altitude around it increased. It instinctively fought against any attempts to remove it from the planet!

Even more amazing was that the artifact seemed capable of differentiating between actual, and simulated altitudes. In hypobaric chambers, its mass to weight ratio remained constant regardless of the simulated altitude; however, an attempt to physically transport the object to a testing facility in New Mexico using a military aircraft proved nearly disastrous!

At ten thousand feet above sea level, cockpit sensors alerted the crew to an unexpected change in the aircraft's weight. Radioing back to the loadmaster, the copilot inquired as to what had changed.

Unable to describe what was happening, the loadmaster simply said, "You should probably come back to check this out for yourself, sir."

Leaving the cockpit, the copilot hustled back to the cargo area to find the loadmaster staring at the shattered wooden pallet beneath the lead lined vault containing the artifact.

"The overload light came on at angels ten," said the loadmaster. "When I came back to take a look, the pallet beneath the vault was buckling, and at angels fourteen, the damn thing shattered!"

The floor beneath the vault was also beginning to buckle when the copilot called out to the pilot "Level off and return to base! We have a serious problem back here!"

The pilot leveled off the aircraft and immediately set course back to Andrews Air Force Base. During their descent, the overload warning lights went out and all the aircraft's instrument panel readings returned to normal.

Once on the ground, the crew was able to remove the vault from the cargo area of the C-5 Galaxy quite easily. The buckling of the floor was extensive and shocking, especially in light of the fact that two M-60 Patton tanks weighing in at fifty tons each, had been transported aboard the same aircraft fewer than twenty-four hours prior to the incident.

It seemed that the more tests were conducted on the artifact, the more cloaked in mystery it became. After undergoing every scientific evaluation known to man, the artifact was deemed unidentifiable with no potential for military applications. Still, just because the United States military couldn't find a practical application for it, didn't mean they'd risk allowing it to fall into the hands of adversaries who might be more successful in unlocking the artifact's secrets.

In light of these concerns, it was assigned a catalog number for storage in a top-secret vault at an unnamed government facility in Nevada.

Airlifting the artifact was absolutely out of the question, so it was loaded into an unmarked military vehicle for the forty-hour journey across the country. By the time they reached Kansas, the artifact had had enough.

That night, on a desolate stretch of highway between Topeka and Junction City, the conversation between the two men inside the tractor-trailer was interrupted by what sounded like a freight train travelling alongside them. Trying to peer beyond the high beams illuminating the dark highway ahead of them, they suddenly felt the vehicle being snatched up into the air! A few seconds later, the truck came crashing back to the ground, but the trailer containing the artifact was swallowed completely by the category F5 tornado which had all but stalked them down the highway!

Both men inside the vehicle were a bit battered, but neither of them had sustained serious injuries despite being lifted nearly ten feet into the air. In fact, they were able to drive the truck all the way to Junction City after they'd searched the surrounding area for their missing trailer.

When the trailer did turn up the next day, it was miles away in Emporia, and the vault which had housed the artifact was still bolted to the floor; however, it had been broken open and the artifact was gone.

Within hours of discovering the mangled trailer, military units descended on the area under the guise of emergency chemical clean-up crews. They painstakingly scoured the area surrounding the wide path cut into the landscape by the tornado, but after several days which yielded nothing, the search was reluctantly called off.

Once again, the artifact was free.

CHAPTER 10

Despite the Department of Defense's best efforts, they were unable to recover the lost artifact. Due to its ability to repel any attempt to tag or otherwise mark it, once it was out of their hands retrieving it would be impossible.

In Emporia, Kansas, cleanup continued long after federal troops had thrown in the towel on their search and recovery mission. The damage caused by a tornado of that magnitude is extensive albeit unpredictable, with its destructive energy matched only by its randomness.

On one side of the street every house was leveled, while directly across that same street, not a blade of grass was out of place on the perfectly manicured lawns of their neighbors.

Jocelyn Pruitt was a teacher at a local elementary school. She was there in her classroom grading papers for the kids enrolled in Summer school when the emergency alert sirens sounded. Fortunately, the school itself was a designated storm shelter with a reinforced concrete bunker in the basement of the building. Unfortunately, her dog Conrad was at home directly in the path of the killer storm.

Inside the bunker with the handful of staff and the building custodian who'd been working late that evening, they could hear the destructive force of the high winds ripping at the building. Even there in the reinforced bunker, the sound was nearly deafening with the tornado raging above them. As they sat there together in the darkness holding hands and praying for deliverance from the storm, the floor beneath them was shaking violently.

Just when they'd begun to accept the possibility that they would never escape the storm alive, the winds subsided, and the lights flickered back on. Looking around at each other, it was obvious they were all surprised to still be there, scared but none the worse for wear.

Once the "all clear" was given by the National Weather Service, Jocelyn immediately ran from the building to the parking lot where she found her car had been pinned beneath a century-old oak uprooted by the tornado. With tears in her eyes and filled with desperation, she continued running towards her house consciously aware of the devastation left in the wake of the storm, and hoping that somehow, Conrad had survived the storm's wrath.

Her lungs were burning as she reached the street where she'd lived for the past decade. The entire neighborhood resembled a war zone without a single house having escaped the destructive force of the tornado. In fact, the street looked more like a lumberyard than a housing suburb.

Upon reaching her address, her horror was complete. Where her modest single-story home previously stood, was now a vacant lot. The house had been razed right down to the foundation. In her mind, she imagined the fear Conrad must have felt. He was so terrified of storms that he would cower beneath her bed at the very sound of distant thunder.

Standing in the middle of the blank concrete slab where her home had been, her heart was breaking. She'd adopted Conrad as a scrappy little puppy which everyone else had overlooked. He was truly a mutt, unkempt and ignored, staring up at her with a look that said, "I know you don't want me either."

He couldn't have been more wrong. Even though Jocelyn had walked away from the cage as he'd expected, she returned within minutes with a collar and leash for him. He was actually scared when she returned with the kennel director. Sometimes dogs would leave with new families, but more often for mutts like him their last walk was out the *other* door. The one leading to the back of the building.

He'd already accepted his fate, curling into a ball with his back to the door. He didn't even bother standing when he heard the cage door opening, expecting the steel cable lasso to be looped around his neck to drag him out of the kennel.

Instead, he heard Jocelyn's soft voice whispering to him, saying "Come on boy, we're going home."

She knelt beside him, gently placing a real collar around his neck which jingled like the one's with the metal tags worn by dogs who got to go home with new families! In an instant, his eyes sparkled back to life and he sprang to his feet. Excitedly, he walked beside her on a real leash right past the other kennels and out the front door.

She named him Conrad after her favorite novelist, Joseph Conrad who's works had actually inspired her to become an educator. Now she stood in the middle of an empty concrete slab looking for the only thing that she felt was irreplaceable... Conrad.

At the rear of the property, the only thing left standing was his doghouse. She'd bought it the day she adopted him, and it was nearly unused, because he'd never spent a single night in it.

Calling out in a shaky voice, she said "Conrad, come on boy. It's time to come home!"

To her sheer and utter amazement, he heard her and peeked cautiously out the door of the doghouse! His relief was obvious as he darted towards her wagging his tail like a helicopter rotor. He joyfully leapt into her arms as she held them out to him, and she pulled him close to her, hugging him tightly.

"Oh my god, Conrad. I'm so happy to see you!" she said with tears of joy streaming down her face. Still holding him in her arms, she walked back toward his doghouse wondering how it had remained untouched in a storm which had completely erased the rest of her neighborhood. Kneeling, she placed him on the ground and he immediately darted into the doghouse, returning seconds later with something in his mouth. Standing on his hind legs with his front paws against her thighs, he presented her with the deerskin pouch containing the artifact.

It had flown into his doghouse seconds before the storm hit, catching his attention, and luring him inside. In fact, he'd slept through the entire storm awakening only upon hearing Jocelyn calling out for him.

Reaching down, she took the hefty little pouch from him as he looked adoringly up at her, tail wagging and panting happily. Merely holding the pouch in her hand sent a surge of energy through her that reverberated in her very core. In an instant, it was clear to her that in her hand, she was holding something with unimaginable power.

Instinctively, Jocelyn tied the straps of the pouch together and slipped it over her head, concealing it beneath her blouse. "Come on Conrad. Let's find a someplace to spend the night. We've got a lot to work out over the next few days," she said.

Conrad happily followed her as they lightheartedly walked down the rubble-strewn streets back towards the middle of town, oblivious to the wreckage. The pandemonium around them was like white noise in the background of a different movie... one in which neither of them played even the slightest of roles.

CHAPTER 11

Standing there in the hotel lobby with nothing to her name except for Conrad and the clothes on her back, Jocelyn smiled to herself as the receptionist completed the registration form.

"There's a $15.00 surcharge for pets, ma'am," said the young woman behind the counter.

"That's fine," replied Jocelyn, placing her credit card on the countertop. "Go ahead and charge it for the entire week."

"Did you have any problems with the tornado that came thru earlier?" asked the receptionist, noting the address on the ID card was only a few blocks away.

"Only material losses," answered Jocelyn. "Everything that matters is right here," she added with a smile.

"Well, here's your room key," said the young woman. "Hopefully, you'll be back in your house before you know it."

"Probably not," replied Jocelyn nonchalantly taking the room key. "But there are other houses and other neighborhoods," she added before walking down the hallway to her room.

Once inside, Jocelyn took a hot shower allowing the water to wash away her anxiety and accumulated tension before retiring between the crisp clean sheets of an unfamiliar bed. Conrad was happy to be wherever Jocelyn was, and dutifully assumed his place on the bed near her feet. They both slept for the remainder of the night and late into the following morning.

When she awakened, the pouch containing the artifact was still around her neck. For someone who'd just lost everything she'd owned, she was surprisingly clear-headed and knew exactly which steps she needed to take in order to get things rolling for herself and Conrad again.

By mid-afternoon, she'd contacted the insurance companies for both her home and automobile, and by the end of the day she already knew exactly when she could pick up the checks from both of them.

Due to the extensive damage caused by the tornado, all Lyon County schools were closed for the coming week, so she and Conrad bought some food and a few articles of clothing, then rented a car, and drove out to Perry Lake for the day. Conrad loved the water and could spend hours exploring the shores of the lake while Jocelyn inspected the artifact more closely away from the prying eyes of intruders.

Removing it from the pouch, she could sense the raw energy emanating from the object as she closed her hand around it. The visions appearing to her were crystal clear, even with her eyes tightly shut.

She could see a Ranger's boat approaching from across the lake and even from a distance she could clearly make out his name engraved into the shining brass nametag over his right shirt pocket. As he drew nearer, Conrad darted to her side barking as the boat reached the shore directly in front of her. She saw the man walking toward her, extending his hand for an introductory handshake.

When she opened her eyes again, there were no boats on the water, and Conrad was nowhere to be seen. Lying back in the tall grass along the shore, she closed her eyes enjoying the warmth of the sun upon her face. The sense of peace she felt was so relaxing that she soon dozed off.

A few minutes later, she was awakened by the sound of an approaching watercraft. Sitting up, she recognized it was a Ranger's boat. As he drew nearer, Conrad darted to her side barking as the boat reached the shore directly in front of her. She smiled as he walked toward her, extending his hand for an introductory handshake.

"Good afternoon, ma'am," he said politely. "I'm..."

"Ranger Madison," Jocelyn interrupted with a smile. "Nice to meet you," she added, shaking his extended hand.

"Have we met?" asked the perplexed Ranger, furrowing his brow as if trying to remember previously making her acquaintance.

"I'm Jocelyn Pruitt, and this is my dog, Conrad," she said cordially.

"And what brings the both of you out to the Lake this lovely afternoon?"

"Well, I'm a teacher over in Emporia, and due to the tornado, Lyon County schools will be closed for the coming week," answered Jocelyn. "I figured it would be a good time for us to get away for a couple of days."

"Glad you're okay, Mrs. Pruitt," said the Ranger earnestly. "It was a category F4, and I heard there was a lot of damage."

"That, Ranger Madison, would be an understatement," replied Jocelyn. "It flattened my entire neighborhood. Good thing I was over at the school grading papers when it hit," she added.

"Your entire neighborhood was destroyed, and you're out here at the lake?" posited the Ranger quizzically.

"Well, it did leave one house standing," said Jocelyn with a smile. "Conrad's house survived without so much as a scratch."

"Well, luck seems to have been on both your sides," said the Ranger shaking his head in amazement. "Have you got family in Emporia, or somewhere to stay until you can get back on your feet?"

"All of my relatives live back east, but we're staying at a hotel in Emporia until we can get an apartment or another house," explained Jocelyn.

"You are mighty calm for someone whose house just got carried off to The Land of Oz," stated Ranger Madison with a curious smile.

"What's a girl to do?" answered Jocelyn. "Worrying about it won't change anything. I've already contacted my insurance agents, and they're taking care of everything," she said, putting on her sunglasses and laying back in the tall grass again.

"The only thing left to do is wait, so we might as well do it here at Perry Lake in the sunshine with the ever-so-charming Ranger Madison," she finished, smiling.

Caught a bit off-guard by her suggestion, Ranger Madison felt his cheeks flushing as he nervously looked down at his wristwatch. "Well, it is getting close to quitting time," he said, scanning the lake for other boats and fishermen. "Looks like we're the only one's out here anyway."

Removing his hat and mirrored sunglasses, he sat down beside her in the grass, enjoying the cool breeze carried up from the water across his face. Suddenly, he remembered the question he'd meant to pose earlier. "By the way... How did you know my name?" he asked.

Pushing down her sunglasses and peering over them with an intriguing smile, she said "I can see into the future."

"You don't say," said the Ranger while smiling back at her.

For the next few hours, they sat there talking about anything and everything that came to mind, never seeming to find a suitable stopping point. Sooner than they realized, the sun had set, and fireflies were lighting up the night sky around them. Conrad was napping on the ground next to Jocelyn having worn himself out traipsing up and down the shores of the lake.

Looking up into the sky, Ranger Madison said, "I've been patrolling this lake for years now, and I've never even noticed how beautiful the stars are from here."

"They're beautiful from everywhere if you can find the time to slow down and notice them," said Jocelyn. "Were it not for a tornado blowing away everything I owned, I'd be curled up on the couch with Conrad and a tub of peppermint and vanilla ice cream."

"I never thought I'd say this, but suddenly that tornado doesn't seem to have been such a bad thing after all," noted Ranger Madison, standing up and putting on his hat again. Reaching down to help her to her feet, he said, "The park's been closed for hours now. Let me walk you back to your car before the Ranger shows up to run you off."

Darting ahead of them, Conrad led the way back up the path to the parking lot where the rental vehicle was parked beneath the streetlight. When the Ranger opened the car door for them, Conrad jumped right in, taking his spot on the passenger seat.

"It's been a pleasure Miss Pruitt," said the Ranger. "Be careful on your way out. The road back to the highway can be a bit tricky at night, and I'd hate for something to happen to you out there."

Extending his hand to her again, he said "Goodnight, Miss Pruitt."

Looking into his eyes, Jocelyn shook his strong hand with a smile before getting into the car, saying "Goodnight, Ranger Madison."

He waited there beneath the streetlight as she drove off toward the parking lot exit. Suddenly, the brake lights lit up the night and the car came to a stop. By the time the car door opened, and Jocelyn got out, he was already running towards her.

It was unclear who started the kiss after they crashed into one another, but after several long minutes in each other's embrace, he said "Brian... My name is Brian."

"I know. Remember... I can see into the future," said Jocelyn, hooking her arm into his as they walked towards the open car door. After another kiss, she slid into the driver's seat and rolled down the window. "Emporia Suites, room 134," she said. Smiling to herself, this time she drove away without stopping despite a near overwhelming urge to do so.

It was nearly 10:00 p.m. when she arrived at the hotel with a very tired but happy Conrad in tow. At the front desk, there were two messages for her from her insurance agents, informing her that both claims had been processed, and that she could come by to pick up the checks the following morning.

After another hot shower in the hotel room, she wrapped one towel around her hair and another around her body before sitting down on the edge of the bed. Toying with the straps at the top of the pouch, she asked herself, "So, what's in store for tomorrow?"

After thinking about it, she said, "Never mind. Surprise me, Mr. Magic Rock. I don't need to know *everything*." With that, she released the pouch around her neck, and finished drying her hair before slipping on the nightgown she'd purchased earlier that day. Conrad was already sound asleep when she crawled between the sheets, waking just long enough to adjust, and fit into the space behind her heels at the foot of the bed.

"Goodnight Conrad. Goodnight Mister Brian Madison," she said aloud before drifting off into a deep restful sleep.

CHAPTER 12

Within two days after receiving the artifact, Jocelyn no longer needed to touch it in order to peek into the *near* future; however, mental excursions into more distant windows of time required a direct physical connection to it.

She decided early on that she would use this new gift only sparingly. She'd always had a sense of adventure and knowing everything which would happen to her far in advance would only serve to dilute the joy of the experience when it actually happened.

A couple of things were obvious to her about the artifact. First of all, it had undoubtedly protected Conrad from a killer storm which claimed the lives of six people and severely injured two hundred more. From the moment she'd placed it around her neck, she felt shielded by a wall of near-impenetrable protection which extended outward, surrounding her and everything she held dear.

Secondly, it seemed to tap into an area of her psyche which had been perceived as her "gift" since childhood. Jocelyn had always been very intuitive, feeling an increased sense of anxiety when something dangerous or unusual was about to happen. The artifact simply amplified her natural proclivity to sense impending danger and odd occurrences, turning them into blockbuster movies inside her mind, complete with names and subtitles. In fact, the visions were so vivid, she had to create a mental tether in order to separate them from reality. It was a simple gesture she used each time she peered into the future. She crossed her fingers.

In reality, that was something she never did, so if inside the dream quest, her fingers were crossed, she could recognize it as a vision into the future no matter how far forward, she ventured.

Finally, the object would shape destiny unerringly in favor of the outcome she most preferred. While it did not allow her to supplant the free will of other people, it did guide her decisions in choosing paths that were most likely to produce the results she desired.

As for Brian... He'd fallen in love with her all on his own, just as he would have had he met her before she'd come into possession of the artifact. The artifact had led her to him, but it had nothing to do with his reaction to her once they met. For Brian, she was funny, intelligent, quick-witted, practical, compassionate, and easygoing. However, she'd been all of those things long before meeting him.

On top of everything else, he found her beautiful. Her hazel eyes burned right through to his soul, and her smile reduced him to a nervous schoolboy, much like those sitting in her classroom at Emporia Elementary. In fact, he'd been unable to think of anything else since meeting her at the lake.

When he showed up at her hotel in a Kansas State Ranger's uniform, his tall, broad-shouldered frame wasn't something easily overlooked! He stood out like a giant sequoia in a stand of red cedars.

It wasn't that there weren't uniformed men in Emporia. Actually, the town was swimming in them since the night of the tornado. Policemen, firefighters, and paramedics seemed to outnumber residents as clean-up efforts were underway. Even the military had deployed National Guard troops to help with search and rescue operations.

Still, the man in the lobby of the Emporia Suites was remarkable in his very presence. He was ruggedly handsome with a clean-shaven angular jawline. His dark brown hair was highlighted by streaks of grey at the temples, providing a stark contrast to eyes, more aquamarine than blue. He removed his flat-brimmed "Smokey the Bear" hat as he came through the door, silencing everything except for the clicking of the taps on his knee-high black leather boots.

The young receptionist behind the check-in counter had already grown weary of the constant buzz of people in and around the hotel. There wasn't a vacant room left in Emporia, yet people continued streaming through the door, completely disregarding the NO-VACANCY sign clearly visible from the street.

Prepared to deliver her now memorized "I'm sorry, but..." speech, the words stuck in her throat when she looked up at the man blotting out the sun coming through the windows in front of her. Although the words formed in her head were clear and intelligent, the garbage tripping over her vocal cords and falling out of her mouth was gibberish as he tilted his head in an attempt to make sense of them.

Behind him, he heard a familiar voice saying, "He's here for us." Turning sharply, he found himself facing a smiling Jocelyn holding a picnic basket, and a tail-wagging Conrad.

Holding his hat with both hands by the rim in front of him, he looked as if he were about to be reprimanded.

"Wow!" she exclaimed. "Now that's what I call a man in uniform!"

Walking up to him, she asked "Is that all for us?"

Clearly taken aback by the double entendre, he held his tongue to keep from sounding like the blathering girl behind him at the reception counter.

"The uniform, handsome," she said smiling. "You look like a walking endorsement for the Rangers Academy."

"Actually, I got here early this morning to help with search and rescue efforts," he managed to say without a stutter. "I have an hour for lunch, and thought I'd come by to see if you'd like to join me."

"I knew you wouldn't have much time, so I stopped by Piggly Wiggly and put together some things for us," she said, holding up the basket. "Being a Ranger and all, I figured you'd be able to find us a nice spot for a picnic."

He had to grin while saying, "Actually, there's a park not far from here that should be perfect."

"Then lead the way Ranger Madison," replied Jocelyn, handing him the basket, and looping her arm into his before the three of them headed out the door of a lobby so quiet, you could have heard a pin drop.

Only a few minutes' walk from the hotel, they arrived at a park which had been untouched by the storm. There was not a broken branch or overturned trash bin in sight. In the shade beneath a large willow tree, they sat enjoying the bread, cheese, lunch meat and fruit while Conrad attempted to catch the squirrels which were always just out of reach in a park full of places for them to hide.

"Jocelyn, you are something else," said Brian. "I can't seem to figure you out, yet you seem to be a step ahead of me in every way."

"Not in every way," replied Jocelyn. "Sometimes, the same wind that blows things away, also brings new things into your life. You just have to be open and willing to embrace them."

"You are right about that," said Brian. "In high school, I was captain of the basketball team. I had a full scholarship to Kansas University, and everyone assumed I'd wind up in the pros one day."

"Why didn't you?" asked Jocelyn.

"Well, I'd always been interested in forestry research and conservation, so I chose that as my major," answered Brian. "It was transformational for me. Once I'd earned my master's degree, basketball couldn't compete with my desire to save the world. One thing led to another, and the next thing you know I'm graduating from the police academy and signing up with the Forestry Service as a Ranger and Conservationist."

"Are you happy?" asked Jocelyn.

"It's a bittersweet happiness," answered Brian. "On the one hand, I can see the effects humans are having on our ecosystem and how our blatant disregard for Mother Nature is slowly killing her. On the other hand, I'm now in a position where I can actually do something about it."

Jocelyn listened intently, admiring his passion and dedication to preserving the Earth for future generations. His entire demeanor changed when he spoke of such things, and with or without the artifact's help, she could see that he was certain to leave a lasting impact on humanity.

"What about you?" asked Brian "Why did you choose Emporia of all the places you could have landed?"

"I don't know really," replied Jocelyn. "I just had a good feeling about it. Emporia literally translates into 'gift from the heaven hand' so how do you top that?" she added with a smile. While tracing his name with her finger along the metal nametag over his pocket, she said "It took a little while, but some gifts are worth waiting for."

Grabbing onto his collar, she pulled his face to hers kissing him. After the kiss, she said "If we don't leave now, you're going to be late getting back to work, and I don't want anyone to think I'm a bad influence on you."

"Far from it," he replied. "This is the first lunch break I've taken in five years, and it was long overdue."

As they packed up their picnic leftovers, Conrad finally abandoned his mission to catch a squirrel, and rejoined Jocelyn and Brian before heading back to the hotel with them. In the parking lot, they stopped at his truck and as he was getting into the driver's seat, she was compelled to cross her fingers for only a second.

Before Ranger Madison could start the engine, Jocelyn's eyes suddenly widened and she said, "When he says 'Let's call it a night. It's getting too dark to see anything.', you have to keep walking. You'll find him beneath an orange door only a few steps further up the hill. He'll be severely dehydrated with a broken right ankle and a sprained left wrist. He's unconscious, so he won't be able to hear you or call out to you, but you have to trust me. He'll be there."

Three seconds later, the radio crackled to life. The voice coming over it said, "Ranger Madison, come in."

"This is Ranger Madison. Go ahead."

"We've got a missing boy out here somewhere. His parents said he was in his bedroom when the tornado snatched half the house up into the air and carried it off to the hills east of town."

"Copy. I'm on my way," said Ranger Madison. "I'll be there in five."

"Promise me! Only a few more steps," said Jocelyn. "He's there. I know it!"

"I promise," said the Ranger. "I trust you."

Seconds later he was speeding out of the parking lot with lights and siren blaring, as Jocelyn and Conrad watched him disappear out of sight.

He reached the search party just as they were ready to begin their sweep of the hillside east of the city. Grabbing a thermos of ice water and a flashlight from his truck, Brian set out with them.

It was very slow-going as they worked their way through the thick forest and tangled underbrush blanketing the hillside. There were so many places a young boy's body could be hidden in that treacherous terrain, so the search party's progress was painstakingly slow even as they raced against time.

Ranger Madison watched as the sun slowly sank toward the hills to the west. Once it dropped below the ridgeline, the entire valley between those two peaks would be cast into darkness, illuminated only by flashlights and the stars overhead.

It was already dark when the call came over the radios. "Let's call it a night. It's getting too dark to see anything."

As the search party ground to a halt and turned to take the long walk back down that dark hillside, Jocelyn's voice reverberated in Brian's ears reminding him of his promise to keep going a few steps further. Ahead, he could make out what appeared to be rubble scattered across the terrain. Pointing his flashlight in that direction, he saw what looked like the remnants of a blue wooden shed propped against a large tree. Walking as fast as possible up the hillside scanning the area for anything orange, he knew he had to be close.

Calling into the darkness, he yelled "Is anybody out there?", knowing the boy was most likely unconscious. Still, nothing remotely close to an orange colored door was anywhere to be seen. Regardless, he charged up the hill toward the blue rubble. Upon reaching it, he realized it wasn't a blue shed at all. It was an old sign painted onto the side of a barn... a blue sign advertising oranges!

Calling out to the retreating search party over his radio, he said "Hey, I've found something up here!"

"Roger that!" came the immediate reply, as several of the flashlights headed down the hillside turned to point back up in his direction.

Lying on the ground next to the deposited wreckage, he dug his way beneath the edge of the wooden barn door weighed down by an actual ton of uprooted trees and rubble deposited there when the tornado dissipated. Wedging his right knee and elbow beneath the wooden door, he was able to lift it just enough to slide his arm deeper into the narrow chasm underneath. With his outstretched fingertips, he finally touched the leg of the little boy buried beneath it.

"Help!" screamed the Ranger at the top of his lungs as the weight of the debris became unsustainable lowering itself onto his entire right side, trapping his outstretched arm and leg beneath it.

"I'm here little guy" said the Ranger, wiggling his fingers reassuringly against the boy's leg. "Hang in there. I'm here with you, and help is on the way. We'll have you out of there in just a minute."

Over and over, he repeated the same lines into the hollow space, even as the pressure crushing his body into the ground forced him to the edge of losing consciousness himself. Finally, several other members of the search party reached them and began clearing away the rubble, digging frantically at the debris with their bare hands. Twenty minutes later, they were able to lift away the heavy barn door which had protected the boy from the falling debris, yet simultaneously buried him alive.

Once the pressure was removed from the Ranger's right side, the sudden rush of blood back into his compressed limbs immediately knocked him out. As his mind sank into blackness, he whispered aloud, "We found him Jocelyn. We found him."

CHAPTER 13

Brian opened his eyes very slowly, dazed and disoriented, and in unfamiliar surroundings. As his blurry vision cleared, he realized Jocelyn was standing at his bedside smiling down at him.

"What do you know? I actually made it to Heaven," he said softly.

"Nope," said Jocelyn. "They wanted you, but I outbid them."

"What was your offer?" asked Brian curiously.

"My life," answered Jocelyn. "I'd have offered more, but the rest of my things are on their way to Oz."

Nodding silently, Brian smiled and closed his eyes, falling asleep again. He knew she'd be there when he woke up and it gave him a deep sense of comfort.

Brian's sacrifice was much greater than anyone had imagined. The injuries he suffered were more severe than those of the boy he'd rescued. The difference being, Brian was very strong and would fully recover, whereas within an hour, the boy would have become the seventh life claimed by the tornado.

The weight of the debris on the door which had pinned him and the boy, gradually overpowered the adrenalin rush which had enabled him to lift and hold the barn door. As that rush faded, over a ton of wreckage slowly drove the right side of the Ranger's body into the ground, separating his shoulder, breaking two ribs, collapsing his lung, and fracturing his tibia.

The conversation with Jocelyn would be his last for the next couple of days as he underwent surgery to repair all of the damage. His doctors kept him in an artificially induced coma to suppress the extreme levels of pain he'd have had to endure while they treated him. However, as expected, everything went exceptionally well and when he awoke three days later, his guardian angel was right there waiting for him.

"Good morning Rumpelstiltskin," said Jocelyn, smiling like she always did when she looked at him. When he tried to sit up, she told him "Hold on Super-Ranger. You need to take it easy for a little while."

"What time is it?" he asked.

"It's 10:00 a.m," she answered.

"What?" he said. "You mean I've been here all night?"

"Well, it's Thursday," she replied. "So, you've been here for three nights."

"I am so fired," he said jokingly.

"It's alright," Jocelyn answered. "I called your boss and told him you'd be absent for a few days. Teacher's orders."

Looking up at her seriously, he asked... "The boy?"

"Daniel," she said. "He's fine. You got to him in time."

"I promised you I would," said Brian, smiling at her.

"Yes, you did," stated Jocelyn. "Now, promise me you'll take it easy for a couple more days, and we can get you out of here by Saturday morning."

"Will you marry me on Saturday afternoon?" he asked, genuinely surprising her!

"Yes," came her one-word answer in response. Leaning over him, she kissed his forehead before adding, "Any Saturday afternoon you choose."

Just then came a soft knock at the door, followed by a nurse peeking in from behind it. "Good morning, Ranger Madison!" she said. "It's nice to see you're awake!"

After taking down his vital signs and administering pain medication through his IV drip, she said "You must be starving. I'll make sure to get some breakfast up here for you right away."

Ten minutes later, Jocelyn was sitting on the edge of his bed feeding him soft scrambled eggs with toast and orange juice. After breakfast, he took her hand saying "I've only known you for five days, and I slept through three of them. How am I already so in love with you?"

"Because I happen to be the girl of your dreams, and you are the man of mine," Jocelyn said with a smile. "No matter how you view it, one plus one will always equal two."

"Is it really that simple?" queried Brian.

"It really is that simple," answered Jocelyn.

Outside the room, another knock at the door interrupted them as the nurse once again appeared, saying "There's someone here who would really, really like to speak with you."

After nodding to her, the nurse stepped aside allowing Daniel to enter Ranger Madison's room in a wheelchair pushed by his mother with his dad right behind them. The boy's left wrist and right ankle were both sporting casts signed by nearly every member of the search party who'd rescued him.

Approaching the Ranger, Daniel said "I just want to thank you for rescuing me, sir, and ask if you wouldn't mind signing my cast."

Smiling broadly, Brian said "You are very welcome, young man, and I'd be honored to sign your cast."

As the boy came nearer, handing Brian a black magic-marker, he said "I could hear you back there, you know... telling me you were out there and wouldn't leave me, and that help was on the way. Before I heard that, I was ready to give up."

"I'm glad you didn't," replied the Ranger after signing the cast and handing him back the marker. "You're a brave young man, and I'm glad I got to meet you."

"Thank you," said the boy before turning to face Jocelyn. "Will you sign it too, Ms. Pruitt?" he asked her.

Wondering if she'd failed to recognize him as one of her students, she hesitantly took the magic marker from him.

"You were the first one there that day," he said. "You told me you were going to send help, and that I had to stay strong."

Slowly shaking her head, she started speaking. "I wasn't there with..."

"Of course, you were!" stated the boy excitedly. "I told you that I was thirsty, and that my arm and leg were hurting. Then you told me to cross my fingers... just like yours were, and you would send help to me right away!"

Looking around the room, everyone was staring at the two of them. Nevertheless, the gratitude in the eyes of Daniel's parents was clear and unmistakable as they hugged both Brian and Jocelyn before departing with their son.

Alone in the room again, Brian said "I've got to admit... we are a great team."

"That, my dear, is undisputed, and I cannot wait to spend the rest of my life with you," Jocelyn replied.

Standing up, she walked over to him, kissing him on the lips before saying, "You, Ranger Madison, need to get some rest, and I need to pick up Conrad from the pet-sitter. I'll be back this evening to check on you before lights out, so don't go wandering off before I get back."

"Not a chance," Brian replied as he watched her walk toward the door.

Before leaving the room, she stopped and turned to face him, saying "I love you Brian... very, very much."

"You'd better," he said with a smile. "Because, this is the last time I'll ever let you walk away from me without chasing you down."

"Promise?" she asked.

"Promise!" he answered without hesitation.

With that, she was on her way, smiling ear to ear.

At the pet-sitter's house, Conrad was on the couch with his paws against the backrest peering out the window when she pulled up to the curb. Once he saw it was Jocelyn getting out of the car, it was impossible to hold him back.

She had long been able to imagine the world through his eyes. She knew what he was thinking and could perceive his emotional state long before they came into possession of the artifact. Now, however, she realized he could also perceive hers. Not in words per se, but she could feel him inside her head, sharing strings of communication with her in a remarkably cognitive manner.

As she turned onto the street where her pet-sitter lived, he'd been in the backyard playing with the other dogs she was taking care of. Mentally, she told him she was almost there, and he immediately broke off his antics with the other dogs and made a beeline to his lookout spot on the couch. When she parked, she could virtually feel him thinking, *"Mama, I can see you!"*, and he was so excited! The instant she made eye contact with him through the window, he bolted for the front door and scooted outside the second the sitter opened it.

By the time she'd walked around to the passenger side of the car, he was there running around her in circles overflowing with pure, unfiltered love for her, and she'd only been gone for four hours. When they came back into the house to pay the sitter, Conrad was beaming with pride that his "person" was there to get him.

Since having the artifact, his behavior toward *her* hadn't changed one iota, but her ability to understand *him* had grown immeasurably. Realizing this, she asked him "What do you think about Brian?"

The barrage of thoughts coming at her were something like, "Happy, picnic, squirrels at the park, shiny boots, nice to

Mama, are we going to the lake again? I like the man who came from the water. Is he coming back? I'm hungry!"

Smiling to herself, she deduced from the emotional eruption that Conrad was going to be just fine with having Brian around.

CHAPTER 14

As predicted; Brian was released from the hospital first thing Saturday morning. A bit more unpredictable was the incredible speed at which he was healing! His fractured shinbone seemed to have miraculously fused itself back together within two days, and the pain from his dislocated shoulder and cracked ribs was relieved with minor doses of acetaminophen. While his surgeon prescribed two weeks of bed rest and instructed him to stay off of his leg and keep it elevated, Brian instinctively knew that would be totally unnecessary. By Saturday afternoon, had he been able to find a Justice of the Peace, he'd have married Jocelyn right then and there.

While Jocelyn was absolutely sure she wouldn't be able to keep him confined to bedrest for two weeks, she did intend to make good use of the next few days to get things organized.

Her house had been a graduation present from her parents. After her father retired, they purchased a house in Florida and signed over the title to the Emporia home to Jocelyn when she received her master's degree. It was definitely an added argument for moving to Kansas, but it was never a house she could see herself living in forever. It was too big, too empty, and filled with too many memories which were, frankly, painful for her.

In December of 1972, both of her parents were killed when their flight from New York to Miami went down in the Florida Everglades. As their only child, the settlement she received from Eastern Airlines was enormous, and combined with the accidental death clause in their life insurance policies, Jocelyn became a very wealthy woman nearly overnight.

Regardless of the financial windfall, she'd worked extremely hard to become and educator, and she really loved teaching kids. However, even though she kept a very low profile and had only a handful of associations outside the workplace, the rumors of her financial status eventually crept out into the daylight. Suddenly, all those guys who'd called her goofy and labeled her a smartass, were finding excuses to call her incessantly, or drop by her house unexpectedly.

While she did get lonely at times, she was certainly not in the market for someone who viewed her as his goofy, smart-assed meal ticket.

It was on a whim that she pulled into the parking lot of the animal shelter. When she saw Conrad, he reminded her so much of herself... a goofy outsider, unwanted and misunderstood by everyone. She had to save him. Now, here she was, shopping for a simple white dress to wear when she married the man of her dreams, while Conrad kept an eye on him to make sure he followed the doctor's orders.

Brian lived at the Ranger's residence inside Perry State Park. Even though the house had a natural rustic exterior, the interior was actually quite modern and well-appointed with three bedrooms and two-and-a-half bathrooms. The living room faced the front of the house and was shaded by the large maple and oak trees which partially concealed the house from the main park thoroughfare. The veranda at the back of the house had a stunning view of Perry Lake with an access path leading right down to the dock where his boat was moored.

After the ninety-minute drive out to the park, Brian was ready to give Jocelyn the grand tour of the house and surrounding property. Jocelyn; however, quickly reminded him of the doctor's orders and told him she was leaving Conrad there with him while she went to a nearby store to buy some groceries and pick up a few other necessities.

"If you need anything you can't reach from the bedroom, tell Conrad and he'll bring it to you," she said before hustling out the door.

For the most part, Brian was content resting in the master bedroom which also had a beautiful view of the lake. Still, he wondered what she meant by "...tell Conrad and he'll bring it to you."

She'd left a glass and a pitcher of ice-water on the nightstand beside the bed along with a plate and some sandwiches. His wheelchair was also parked within arm's reach and his slippers were right beside the bed where he could slip into them easily if necessary. He was wondering what else he could ask for, when he heard the mail being dropped in through the mail slot at the front door.

"Hey, Conrad."

Conrad immediately sat up at the foot of the bed as if waiting for further instructions.

"Can you bring me the mail, buddy?"

Without hesitation, Conrad jumped off the bed onto the floor, his claws clicking against the linoleum as he scurried down the hallway to the front door. Thirty seconds later, he jumped back onto the foot of the bed with four envelopes in his mouth, which he casually dropped on Brian's lap before circling three times and lying down again, facing the door.

Brian's jaw dropped in disbelief! Conrad had responded to his request in such a matter-of-fact way, it seemed almost boring to him. Maybe he'd try something a bit more challenging this time.

"Hey, Conrad," said Brian.

Conrad sat up again, eagerly awaiting further instructions.

"Can you bring me the mustard from the table in the kitchen?" he asked.

Once again, Conrad disappeared from the foot of the bed clicking off down the hallway. In a flash he was back, hopping back up onto the foot of the bed with the bright yellow bottle of mustard in his mouth! This time, he didn't lay down facing the door again, but waited to see what else he could get for Brian.

By the time Jocelyn returned to the house and crept into the room, it was hard to see the bed because of all the clutter covering it. There were socks and towels, an oven mitt, a baseball glove, three different colored t-shirts, a couple of magazines, a flashlight, and Brian's uniform hat strewn across the bed. Conrad was lying on the bed with his head on Brian's lap dozing while Brian ate his sandwich. The moment he saw Jocelyn in the doorway, he sprang to his feet and rushed to her excitedly jumping into her arms and licking her face.

"Where on Earth did you find that dog?" Brian asked with a wide grin on his face. "He is amazing, and probably smarter than half the people I know!"

"Conrad is a kindred spirit," answered Jocelyn. "I found him at the animal shelter in Emporia, and we connected immediately. He's been with me ever since," she concluded, stroking his head, and scratching his chin.

"Well, you were right. He brought me everything I asked for, but he wouldn't let me leave the room."

"Doctor's orders," replied Jocelyn, smiling. "Now, I've got a few things to put away, then I'm making dinner for you before I head back to Emporia."

"That's going to be one long dinner, because there's no way I'm letting you drive all the way back to Emporia tonight," said Brian. "I've got two spare bedrooms and more than enough space here for you to store all of your belongings. Besides, I'm sure Conrad will be happier here, than in some cramped hotel room."

"Yes Sir, Ranger Madison," replied Jocelyn, saluting him before making her way back down the hallway and into the kitchen.

It only took a few minutes before she had the house smelling like someone actually lived there. It was a simple meal. Tossed salad and spaghetti Bolognese was something her mother would make for her dad when he wanted comfort food. Somehow, it seemed appropriate for a first home-cooked meal with Brian.

"That was amazing, Jocelyn... *You* are amazing," said Brian after finishing two large helpings of spaghetti.

"Call me inspired," said Jocelyn. "Now, let's get you back to bed."

"I'm actually feeling much better. It's like being around you makes me heal faster."

Looking into those shockingly blue eyes, Jocelyn said, "I need to show you something." Walking toward him, she swung her leg over his lap and sat down facing him. Without losing eye contact, she unbuttoned the top three buttons of the sundress she'd bought earlier that day especially for him. When he opened his mouth to speak, she placed a finger against his lips, saying "Shhhh..." before lifting the pouch containing the artifact from beneath the dress.

"One week ago, right before the storm hit Emporia, Conrad found this in his doghouse. Somehow, it protected him from the tornado that wiped the rest of our subdivision completely off of the map," she explained. "Afterwards, he brought it to me and the moment I touched it; I could feel myself bonding with it."

Taking his hand, she let the full weight of the pouch rest against his palm. "This thing must weigh five pounds!" he exclaimed.

"Yet, when I'm wearing it around my neck, it seems as light as a feather," she replied. "And, it helps me visualize things which haven't even happened yet."

"That's how you knew about the boy, isn't it?" Brian said.

"Yes," answered Jocelyn. "It's also how I knew your name before we ever met. It doesn't give me control over other people or anything, but it does guide me in my choices, and helps me to understand and help others. I believe it also bonded with Conrad to some extent, because now he can accurately understand my thoughts, and apparently he understands yours too."

Still supporting the artifact's weight in his hand, Brian asked "Do you know where it came from, or what it's made of?"

"I can sense it traveled a very long way to get here, and it has passed through many different hands, but aside from that, I can only tell what it does with me, and even *that* is still a work in progress," explained Jocelyn.

Continuing, she said "It's also the reason you are healing so fast. Whenever I'm around you, I can feel it reaching out to repair your body and give you strength."

"That is amazing," said Brian.

"It knows that I love you, and since you are important to me, it instinctively protects you as well. Obviously, its bond to Conrad also extends to you. That's why I left him with you today, and it's also the reason he can understand exactly what you ask him to do."

Looking into Brian's eyes, she continued "While you were sleeping in the hospital, I placed my hand on your broken leg, and I could feel the energy flowing into your body and healing your fractured tibia. It left me a bit drained at first, but after a little while I felt fine, and I am positive that your fracture has completely healed."

"I can feel that too," said Brian.

"When I kissed you before I left to go shopping, I placed my hand on your shoulder for only a moment, and I could feel it healing miraculously beneath my palm," said Jocelyn.

"Now that I think about it, my shoulder hasn't been hurting at all since then, and even my ribs are only mildly sore now," noted Brian.

Slowly lifting his t-shirt, Jocelyn placed her left hand over his broken ribs. For a moment, she had a mild sense of vertigo but when it passed, she looked into Brian's eyes and said, "It's healed you."

Wide eyed, Brian replied, "I felt it. The pain and swelling are completely gone now! It's like nothing ever happened to me!"

Sliding off of his lap, Jocelyn once again stood in front of him. "I've got something else to show you now," she said, unbuttoning the three remaining buttons on her new sundress, and letting it fall to the floor. Beneath it she was naked.

Without a word, Brian stood up and scooped her into his strong arms kissing her passionately as she clung to him with both of her arms around his neck. The kiss continued while he carried her down the hallway to the bedroom, they'd vacated less than an hour earlier.

In the living room, Conrad was on the couch with his paws against the backrest, staring out the window... completely engrossed and amazed by the sheer number of squirrels in Brian's front yard.

CHAPTER 15

Two weeks after the storm had carved a thirty-eight-mile-long path right through the middle of their lives, Emporians were gradually getting back to something close to normal. The fallen trees and downed power lines had been removed, and neighborhoods were cleared of unwanted debris blown in by the tornado.

The flood of first responders and National Guard troops had withdrawn, and the community, for the most part, had picked up where it had left off before the storm. For someone passing through or visiting for the first time, nothing would have seemed out of the ordinary at all.

After only nine days, Brian had talked the doctor into rescheduling his follow up appointment for sooner, and to the doctor's utter amazement, all of his injuries had healed completely.

"I'm not sure how you did it, but you seem to have defied the limitations of human biology," stated the doctor. "I'm clearing you for work, but take it slowly and, at the first sign of pain or discomfort, call me or come by right away."

"You've got it, Doc," Brian replied before heading out to join Jocelyn and Conrad in the waiting room. Ten minutes later, they were parking at the Lyon County courthouse for an appointment with the Justice of the Peace.

After getting out of his truck, he walked around to open the passenger side door for Jocelyn. While she was still seated, he asked "Are you sure you're ready for this, Sweetheart?"

"I've never been surer about anything," said Jocelyn before asking, "What about you? Are you ready to give up the bachelor life for me?"

Smiling, Brian reached into his jacket pocket and removed a small box. Inside it there were three rings. Two of them were simple golden bands. The other was a classic princess-cut diamond ring.

Removing the engagement ring, he knelt there in the asphalt parking lot taking her hand in his. "This may be history's shortest engagement ever; but, will you be my wife, Jocelyn Pruitt?"

Getting out of the car and smoothing her new white dress down the sides with her hands, she looked down at him and said "Yes, Brian Madison. I'd be a fool not to."

Brian slid the ring onto her finger before standing up and kissing her. "Then, let's get married!" he said, taking her hand in his as they dashed off to the courthouse together.

Inside the courthouse, a few of Jocelyn's co-workers were waiting with Brian's boss and a couple of his fellow rangers from the park. When Jocelyn turned to look at him in amazement, he said with a smile "I made a few phone calls while you were out shopping."

"I was wondering how you came up with the rings so quickly," said Jocelyn, raising an eyebrow.

"Sweetheart, I bought these rings the morning after I met you out at the lake," said Brian sheepishly. "I was going to ask you for your hand that day, but as I recall, we got a bit sidetracked."

Words could not have described the love she felt for him at that moment. Just when she thought he'd maxed out the meter on adorable, he'd surprised her again.

Seconds later, they were inside the office of the Justice of the Peace surrounded by their smiling colleagues as they committed their lives to one another. The actual ceremony was a blur to both of them, as everything around them faded quietly into the background. After their pronouncement, they made their way down the courthouse steps in a rain of applause and rice.

The words JUST MARRIED were painted across the rear window of Brian's truck with canned Christmas snow, and the train of tin cans attached to the bumper followed them noisily down the road as they exited the parking lot on the way to their long, beautiful future together.

While the artifact's protective energy field was ever-present around Jocelyn, Brian, and Conrad, their lives were never dependent upon it in any way. They made wise decisions, they took care of each other, and they were never wasteful. Above all, they deeply loved one another, and the power of that love absolutely dwarfed anything the artifact could have created or propagated.

Jocelyn transferred to Perry Elementary after completing Summer School for her students in Emporia. While everyone was sad to see her leave, they were all happy that she'd found her perfect match in Brian, and her new job was only twenty minutes from the park.

After the new school year started, Conrad spent most of the day with Brian. Whether patrolling the park in his official vehicle, or the shores of Perry Lake in his boat, Conrad seemed to believe it was his responsibility to take care of Brian while Jocelyn was working. Within a month, Conrad was a regular fixture among the employees and guests who frequented the park.

He quickly learned the ropes when it came to Brian's daily routines, helping him open the public facilities each morning, and complete the evening checklists for all of them when they closed each night. At times, Brian felt that, if Conrad had possessed thumbs, he could have handled almost every aspect of being a park ranger all by himself! In any case, Conrad loved the park, and everyone who worked there or visited regularly, loved Conrad.

Working with new children in a new school was so fulfilling to Jocelyn. It gave her a sense of rebirth after having her slate blown clean by the tornado. In losing everything, she'd gained so much more than she had ever lost, and "the man who came from the water" had given her so much more than a new last name.

Their first child, Richard was born forty-five seconds before their second child, Nicolas, two years to the day of their meeting at Perry lake. The two perfectly healthy baby boys were the spitting image of Brian, and the intellectual reflections of Jocelyn. Even before they were able to speak, you could see them carrying on mental conversations with one another and coordinating their efforts to get what they wanted.

Conrad was constantly there watching over them, always a step ahead of them in their attempts to trick him, even when being double-teamed. He loved the boys very much, but he wouldn't hesitate for a second to rat on them to Jocelyn and Brian if they were up to mischief.

Nevertheless, Conrad was their favorite thing in the whole world and his energy and willingness to chase them, and anything they threw for him, was the reason they slept in exhausted peace each night.

Their connection to him was separate and distinctly different than the one they had with Brian and Jocelyn. Conrad was their mutual confidant and had kept them from making bad decisions on more than one occasion.

Two years after the twins were born, Rebecca made her appearance on the Madison family stage. From the moment she was born, she was daddy's little girl, with Brian firmly wrapped around her little finger.

Conrad was beside himself with joy, because he was always the honored guest at each of her tea parties... which always included real cookies, even if the tea was imaginary. Having his fur braided and his toenails painted was a small price to pay for such an honor, and he never complained in even the slightest of ways.

Rebecca not only looked as if she were cloned from Jocelyn, she was also blessed with her mother's "gift" of precognition. It manifested itself in small ways at first, but by the time she was five, she could tell you who was calling before the phone even rang. Furthermore, she didn't require the power of the artifact in order to do it.

For Brian and Jocelyn, it seemed as if Rebecca had genetically inherited her mother's abilities at their levels as enhanced by the artifact. Using them also came naturally to her, and with Jocelyn there to guide and encourage her development, she never saw her gift as something either to be ashamed of, or to boast about.

While she did occasionally tell her brothers if the girls, they liked were actually interested in them or not, most of the time those answers were obvious to everyone else anyway. Both of her brothers were tall, intelligent, and very handsome. Of course, lots of girls were interested in them!

One night in July of 1990, after the boys had fallen asleep, Conrad crept out of their room and down the hallway to Brian and Jocelyn in the master bedroom. When he hopped up onto the bed, Jocelyn woke up and scooped him toward her, wrapping her arms tightly around him.

Without a word, Brian rolled over to face them both, scooting closer. Even in the darkened room, he could see the tears streaming down Jocelyn's face.

It was only a minute or so before Bee, Nick, and Rick joined the intimate huddle on their parents' bed, wordlessly cuddling up around Conrad as he spent his final night, loved beyond all measure, and surrounded by his amazing family.

CHAPTER 16

Brian and Jocelyn remained in the Ranger's residence at Perry State Park until 1996, when he retired after having been promoted to park superintendent nearly twenty years earlier. Jocelyn remained in the public-school system doing what she loved... shaping the lives of future leaders, educators, and public servants. It was also her way of dealing with "empty nest" syndrome after Rick, Nick, and Bee went off to college.

After Brian's retirement, Jocelyn was appointed by the State Board of Education to the position of Commissioner of Education. Her common-sense approach to educating children, developing comprehensive lesson plans, and connecting the developing minds of students to their study material in unconventional ways, was elemental in revolutionizing the state's educational system.

The twins were both accepted to Stanford University in 1994, and even though Jocelyn would have liked for them to attend a college closer to home, she was at least comforted by the thought that Rick and Nick would be close to one another. Even though they'd never been co-dependent upon each other, their bond of sibling rivalry was beneficial to both of them, keeping them grounded and focused on their studies.

Since her early childhood, Bee had been a stargazer, fascinated by the infinite possibilities and sheer vastness of space beyond our solar system. She possessed a natural curiosity for things yet unknown and looked to the heavens for knowledge and understanding. At times, she felt as if the stars were communicating with her, and in 1996, she was accepted to Harvard University where she studied astronomy and astrophysics.

Even though Rebecca's choice of universities took her far away in the opposite direction of her brothers, she and Jocelyn shared a unique psychic bond which was unaffected by time and space. They spoke regularly with one another, and always felt connected.

One night while she and Brian were curled up on the couch watching the *Sunday Night Movie*, Jocelyn felt a powerful jolt run through her entire body. When Brian looked over at her, it appeared she was having a seizure! As he sprang to his feet to run for the telephone, she grabbed his arm, saying "No!"

After a moment, the episode passed and she said, "Call Bee."

Before he could even reach the phone, it was ringing, and Rebecca's caller I.D. was flashing on the LCD screen.

When Brian answered, before he could even say a single word, Rebecca asked "What's wrong with Mom?!" Wordlessly, he handed the phone to Jocelyn.

After taking the phone from Brian, Jocelyn said "Bee, I need you to come home right away. I have something important to give you, and we haven't got much time."

"I'm already on the way to the airport, Mom," she said. "I'll be there in just a few hours."

After she hung up the phone, Brian asked, "What's going on Sweetheart? For a moment, you were pale as a sheet!"

"I'm fine, my love," Jocelyn said. "I'll explain everything when Bee gets here, but we need to leave soon, because her flight will be arriving early."

As predicted, Rebecca's plane landed only a few minutes after Brian and Jocelyn reached the airport in Topeka. She exited the terminal with no luggage, and only her purse and a handbag thrown over her shoulder. She was met with kisses and hugs at the curbside pickup point by both her parents before they all got into the car and headed home.

The ride was an unusually quiet one as Jocelyn and Bee were communicating without words between the front and back passenger seats. Brian was well-acquainted with their direct lines of communication to one another and allowed them to connect without interrupting them.

Back at the house, they all sat at the dining room table together as Jocelyn began to explain what she'd experienced. Despite having grown up and spending over eighteen years nearly welded to her mother's hip, Rebecca never even knew about the artifact. Jocelyn had worn it around her neck without taking it off since Conrad brought it to her back in 1974, and now it was time for her to pass it on.

Removing it from beneath her blouse, she lifted it over her head before taking Rebecca's hand and placing the pouch in her palm. Bee's eyes rolled back into her head as her body immediately stiffened, and she began to shake from head to toe.

Brian resisted the urge to intervene, understanding that something extremely important was happening between Jocelyn and his little Bee. After a few seconds, the episode passed just as it had with Jocelyn earlier, and when she opened her eyes she was as pale as her mother had been.

"This has been developing for over a billion years," began Jocelyn. "This object... this artifact, has been making its way through time and space in order to be here... right here, right now."

With Brian and Bee listening carefully, she continued. "It has been learning and accumulating knowledge and experience the entire time it's been here. From centuries spent protecting Native American societies near Lake Huron, to watching the growth of the agricultural industry in North America, it learned to shield those who've held it."

"It learned the lessons of betrayal from those willing to lie and sacrifice the lives of others in order to regain control of the energy it alone possessed."

"It observed without intervening as men bought and sold other men for profit, attempting to make sense of the inhumane concept of subjecting fellow human beings to various forms of human atrocity," she continued. "However, it also learned the selfless nature of those who heal others, despite them being labeled as enemies due to different social ideologies. It's come to realize that evil is a trait found within the souls of all men, held in check only by the goodness also found in them," Jocelyn explained.

"It learned the concept of hubris by those who felt entitled to power and influence, without having actually earned it, and witnessed the ease of which the very thing enabling their elevated status could be abandoned as unnecessary."

Jocelyn seemed to be traveling through time as she recounted the lessons the artifact had accumulated as she continued. "It learned the necessity of envisioning a future and setting goals beyond one's self in order to add meaning to life beyond the accomplishment of a single objective. It also knows the consequences of being steeped in evil, and the destiny that will unerringly find those who embrace it, with or without the artifact."

"Over the centuries, it came to understand the importance of time and the value of cherishing the human experience every second of every day, realizing that one second, no matter how far it is stretched, is still one second. In the same sense, it learned that failure to adapt to change can leave a society holding onto dreams and visions which, without them realizing it, have long turned to dust in their very hands."

Immersed in the artifacts energy, Jocelyn prodded forward, explaining "It experienced first-hand, the bureaucratic thirst for knowledge and the entrenched desire for humans to analyze and understand any and everything, without accepting that some things lie outside and beyond the limits of human understanding. Being held in captivity and examined for so long, it also came to recognize how some humans would rather lock something away from everyone, rather than allow others the opportunity to discover the secrets that they, themselves, had been unable to."

"It even recognizes and understands that all living things are connected in their desire for love and acceptance, and that we all sense fear and sorrow in the same way, even if we express it differently," said Jocelyn with a smile while thinking of Conrad. "And, through us... our little family, it learned the meaning of unconditional love, acceptance, and sacrifice without passing judgement."

Taking Rebecca's hands in hers, firmly pressing them around the pouch containing the artifact, she said "The artifact has passed this knowledge on to you, Bee, because your destiny is perhaps one of the most important that mankind will ever face." As she continued, a seriousness gripped her that neither Brian nor Bee had ever seen in Jocelyn before.

"Each shaman had the gift of being protectors for their people. Those traders who benefitted from the power of the artifact indirectly, all had the gift of understanding and providing for the needs of a community. The young slave had the gift of retaining his sense of humanity and healing others, even when stripped of his dignity by lesser men," explained Jocelyn before continuing.

"The unnamed murderer who lacked reverence for life learned the tragedy of his ways when he was cursed to forfeit his own life by reaping the pain and horror he had sown. The young boy in England possessed the gift of manipulating the progression of time by accelerating or slowing it with merely a thought, and our little Conrad was gifted with telepathy that allowed him to communicate with every living being on Earth."

"My gift since childhood," continued Jocelyn "has been precognition, allowing me to skip forward in time to see what lies ahead."

"Each shaman, the traders, the slave, the watcher, the serial killer, the boy, Conrad, and I… each had a different supernatural gift." Pausing for emphasis, Jocelyn held Bee's hands firmly before saying, "You, my heart of hearts… *you* have them all!"

Bee looked down at the pouch in her hands and could clearly see the energy surrounding it. She could visualize the lives of everyone who'd touched, held, or worn the artifact even briefly. "But, why now?" she asked, afraid of the vision forming in her mind that she already knew was true."

"This tiny artifact is just a small piece of an even greater object which began its journey at the same time, millions of years ago," Jocelyn explained. "It was the second of three objects on the same, unwavering, and unaltered course. While traveling at different velocities when they were jettisoned from the collapsing dark star where they originated, the trajectory for all of them is exactly the same."

Jocelyn paused momentarily, terrified that speaking the words aloud might actually accelerate the inevitable. Resolutely, she continued. "The first piece was the size of Manhattan when it struck the Earth millions of years ago, resulting in the global extinction of the entire dinosaur species. This tiny fragment started out with a diameter of six-hundred miles, clearing a wide path through asteroid fields and other space debris, fragmenting, and shedding mass before entering Earth's atmosphere and burning off even further. When it hit the upper atmosphere, it was only the size of a cantaloupe, but even at that size, it survived Earth's protective barrier and struck the planet. It was still the size of an orange when it burrowed into the glacier where it cooled and compressed for thousands of years down to this," Jocelyn said, holding and shaking Bee's hands with the artifact clutched in them. "This thing is the size of an olive and it weighs nearly six pounds."

Continuing slowly, Jocelyn said "The final piece of that cosmic projectile is still on its way to Earth... and it's the size of Kansas."

CHAPTER 17

It didn't take a rocket scientist to understand that an object of that size and density striking the Earth would be the end of everything. Not even microbes would survive such a devastating cataclysmic event.

It would; however, take a team of rocket scientists, astrophysicists, engineers, chemists, and architects to prevent that deadly third strike from ending all life on the planet. Even with a team of such exceptional minds working on a solution around-the-clock, it would take a decade to develop a plan, implement it, finance it, build it, and have it in place in time to intercept the massive object racing undetected towards Earth.

Furthermore, it would need to be intercepted as far from Earth as possible to make sure that even the smallest pieces of it could be either destroyed or redirected away from our planet. Otherwise, that thing out there would be knocking at the door in ten years, adding a period to the end of the human evolutionary chapter.

Seated at the kitchen table she'd grown up with, Rebecca asked Jocelyn, "How am I supposed to stop this!? I'm just one individual on a planet of seven billion people. Surely, there is someone else who..."

"Rebecca..." interrupted Jocelyn. "The artifact chose you. You know as I do, that this thing has never executed a random act. Everything it has done up to this point has been for a purpose," she said. "It has been searching, learning, and evaluating the evolving human race since it got here. Had it not concluded that we're worth saving, it would simply have remained on a shelf in some anonymous military warehouse until its big brother arrived to clean up the mess we'd made of the world."

"It chose you," continued Jocelyn, "because you're the only one who actually can save us, and it knows that!"

"But I don't know how!" exclaimed Rebecca, in tears.

Jocelyn calmly took the pouch and slipped it over Rebecca's head, draping it around her neck. Wiping the tears from her daughter's cheeks, she said "It knows how, and it will guide you in making the right decisions... The decisions that are necessary to save everyone." Hugging her daughter, Jocelyn added "I have seen your father and I in excellent health and enjoying our grandchildren far into the future. That future wouldn't be possible if not for you, Bee. You have already saved the world, Sweetheart. The artifact only needs to show you how you did it."

"But why couldn't it have just shown you?" Rebecca asked.

"Because I am not a Nobel Laureate, Bee. You are, and you have many more 'gifts' than I have," explained Jocelyn. "You will need them to face what lies ahead of you, so trust in the artifact, but above all... trust in yourself. The artifact already does."

Rebecca nodded silently, looking down at the table. Wearing the artifact around her neck, its weight was barely even noticeable, and she could already feel it bonding with her. While there were still so many questions and so much work to be done, she was no longer afraid to face them, realizing her mother's words were true.

That night, she slept soundly, waking the next morning with a plethora of new knowledge imparted to her by the artifact. She could already see the steps which needed to be taken, now all she had to do was convince a few hundred people she didn't even know yet, to work with her on solving a problem they didn't even realize they had.

When Brian and Jocelyn dropped Rebecca off at the airport later that morning, they both hugged her, reassuring her that there was nothing she couldn't accomplish once she'd put her mind to it. After the hug, Brian told her "Now, get out there and save the world, Little Bee!", smiling after her as she headed into the terminal with an obvious determination to her gait.

Before she even boarded the plane, she'd already spoken with two Harvard professors, and a fellow astronomer and astrophysicist from a private observatory near her home in Boston. The first order of business would be to convince other respected scientists and advisors to NASA and the United States Department of Defense, that the threat was real and urgent. This was, after all, something which threatened the very existence of life on Earth, and there was no time for procrastination or excessive bureaucracy.

Rebecca flew first-class on the way back to Boston in order to utilize the time and familiarize herself with the nature of the artifact. Surprisingly, even the metal detectors and TSA body scanners failed to detect the artifact when she passed through the security checkpoint at the airport. Furthermore, unlike the near disastrous attempt by the military to use air transportation, the artifact was quite docile in Rebecca's possession. Even at thirty-five-thousand feet, its gravitational mass never fluctuated.

Removing the pouch from beneath her sweater, she clutched it firmly in her hand. Unlike her mother, she didn't need to place it directly in her palm to bond with it. Rebecca's senses were much more attuned to the artifact, and the information it revealed to her was infinitely more detailed than what Jocelyn had learned from it.

The artifact around her neck was not the second to strike the Earth. It was, in fact, the third. Furthermore, this was not some random asteroid which happened to strike the planet by accident. It's presence here was absolutely intentional. In fact, it wasn't an asteroid at all. It was a projectile—a glorified bullet fired at the Earth from a galaxy away.

During the flight, the attendants attempting to get her attention believed she was sleeping, but actually, the informational trance in which she was submerged, was force-feeding her facts and data which were crucial in preparing the measures necessary to avoid an extinction level event.

The first artifact preceded the age of the dinosaur, and had served as a measuring device, which allowed some extra-terrestrial entity to evaluate the development of the Earth's most dominant species. It was the sole key to either the survival of the species or the absolute obliteration of it. Unfortunately, dinosaurs were unable to evolve to a point where they could unlock the secrets of the artifact. Having failed to do so, the second projectile homed in on the first one as if it were a targeting beacon.

The resulting impact eradicated the dinosaurs, clearing the slate while simultaneously planting the elemental and biological seeds for a new species to emerge... Mankind. Once that process was underway, the third projectile, now dangling from Rebecca's neck, was sent to evaluate the advancements of this new dominant species, and if they also failed, the fourth projectile, now rapidly approaching Earth, would once again clear the slate for the next species to emerge.

As mankind evolved, they were clandestinely observed for thousands of years, and while those observers were forbidden from physically intervening, they did leave clues which an evolving species would come to understand over the course of their development. If they were able to crack the code and make sense of the clues intentionally left within their grasp, the knowledge contained within the artifact would reveal to them, the steps necessary to ensure the continuation of all life on Earth, and allow them to remain the dominant species.

In this deep mental trance, Rebecca's mind was racing. She was already assembling teams of experts who would need to work together with other teams in order to complete each stage of this grand survival operation. She knew exactly what must be done. Now, all she had to do was convince the rest of the world to work together in saving the planet... something which, in mankind's entire history, they had never been able to do.

Rebecca awoke from her educational reverie just as the captain announced that they were on their final approach to Logan International Airport in Boston. The moment the wheels of the aircraft touched down, she was on the phone with another key individual who, although essential to the success of this mission, was going to be a tough "sell" to the rest of the team.

His name was Adam Levinson, and for decades, he'd been preaching his end-of-the-world sermon to anyone who would listen. For the most part, he'd been publicly ignored even while making accusations of a coverup by the United States Government regarding the existence of extraterrestrial life beyond our solar system.

In truth, he'd been uncomfortably close to reality in many of his predictions which made several high-level public officials uneasy, even though they couldn't officially acknowledge their trepidation without divulging highly classified information. Instead, they labeled him a lunatic, while secretly keeping him under close observation.

Mr. Levinson wasn't fooled by the governmental smokescreens, and vociferously professed that his knowledge and disclosure of sensitive information was necessary if we were to survive the apocalyptic events facing mankind in the not-so-distant future. In truth, there thousands of people around the globe who found his assertions to be plausible if not outright factual.

While his messages, figuratively shouted from the rooftops, were a nuisance to many federal agencies, he was much too high-profile an individual to simply eliminate or make disappear. Suddenly, those agencies who'd worked hardest to marginalize him, were going to have to deal with his assertions on a very real level, and it was going to be as volatile as tossing a bucket full of ping-pong balls into a room full of cocked mousetraps.

While Rebecca was never one prone to fall victim to mass hysteria surrounding theories like the Y2K societal meltdown, there was one date which appeared in her visions as a recurring milestone. It had been viewed by many as a day to end all days based on the historical Mayan Calendar. Now it was virtually screaming into Rebecca's inner ear.

The date of the fourth impact would be December 21st, 2012.

CHAPTER 18

Rebecca's first meeting was at the private observatory of Professor Doctor Heinrich Schultz. While he evaluated every astronomical theory presented with a pragmatic, fact-based approach, he was also willing to acknowledge the x-factor... that element which, as yet, had eluded mankind's intellectual grasp.

The two Harvard professors she'd spoken with, were both leaders in their fields. Professor Doctor Matthias Novak was a brilliant chemist working on groundbreaking fuel technologies to increase the payload of satellite deployment vehicles, by using less fuel and more efficient propulsion systems. Professor Doctor Stephan Wagner had written several dissertations on harnessing dark matter to create magnetic and gravitational propulsion systems for use in deep-space exploration vehicles.

The fifth person was Adam Levinson. While he was neither a professor nor a doctor, when it came to extraterrestrial research and documentation, there was no one with a more comprehensive database of human/alien contact, nor anyone more qualified to interpret the plethora of evidence which pointed to extraterrestrial intervention in the evolution of the human species. While many of his critics attempted to paint him as an aluminum-foil helmeted lunatic, his evidence was compelling and, in many cases, unchallenged and irrefutable.

Rebecca realized immediately that she'd chosen the right people to create the foundation of the team. She arrived fifteen minutes early, just as everyone else did. While they all stood there in the parking lot curiously eyeing each other, Rebecca made the introductions without breaking her stride as she walked past them and approached the front door of the observatory. Professor Doctor Schultz was standing in the open doorway to greet them as they approached.

Forgoing the small talk, Rebecca jumped right into the meat of the matter, saying "Gentlemen, we have an intergalactic projectile headed towards Earth. Unless we can stop it out there, it will impact Earth on December 21st, of 2012 and everyone in this room, or any other room on this planet will die."

Looking around, she knew her words were taken seriously by everyone as she continued. "This projectile hasn't been detected by anyone yet because no one is even looking for it. I know where to look for it and how to find it. What I don't know is how to reach it before it reaches us, or how to deal with it when we do."

The silence in the room spoke volumes as Rebecca continued, saying "The answers to all of these questions are here in this room, and we need to unlock them, so we can convince all the stuffed shirts at NASA, the Department of Defense, and in Washington DC to get off of their asses, and help us save the world."

"And where do we find this... projectile?" asked Heinrich. "I have the precise locations of every moving object in our solar system which will come within one-hundred-fifty million kilometers of the Earth, and I know of no such projectile."

"This object has not yet entered our solar system, Heinrich," responded Rebecca. "If we wait for it to appear before we act, it will be too late... far, far too late," she added. "This is not a random asteroid. It's an extraterrestrial bullet, fired at the Earth from a different galaxy to test our evolutionary progress. Its sole purpose is to evaluate the state of human evolution and determine if we have advanced enough as a species to be welcomed into the intergalactic community of worlds. It's a test we simply cannot fail, for if we do, we are all lost."

"Can you tell us how to find it?" asked Stephan.

"Yes, I can," answered Rebecca. "I can tell you exactly when and where it will appear, but we will need your expertise in order to reach it," she added.

"But my work is still largely theoretical. There are gaps in my research which will require solutions before my dark matter and gravitational propulsion systems can be deployed," Stephan replied.

"As I've already mentioned," said Rebecca, "all of the solutions are here in this room. In your case, Mr. Levinson has them."

"I have them?" asked Adam. "I would definitely know if I were holding the missing link to utilizing dark matter in propulsion systems."

"Adam," replied Rebecca, "You've had them for many years. In fact, you also have the missing elements that Matthias will need to perfect his fuel formula and their related deployment vehicles."

"And where has Mr. Levinson been holding this critical research?" asked Matthias. "Wouldn't we have noticed if he'd been involved in the development of such complex formulas?"

"I didn't say he developed them. I said he *has* them," answered Rebecca. "Extraterrestrial intelligence has been given to us overtly over the past several decades, and while Mr. Levinson compiled the evidence, he didn't actually recognize their significance, just as neither of the rest of us did."

Reaching into her satchel, she retrieved several pages of photos downloaded from Adam's official website. "These images are of crop circles in Great Britain. This one in particular shows the molecular composition of an incredibly efficient rocket fuel. I'm sure if Matthias compares them with the molecular structure of the fuel formula, he's been working on, it will advance his research significantly!"

The look on Matthias's face made it apparent that Rebecca's hypothesis had been spot on! The structure of the crop circles was nearly a perfect overlay of the molecular diagram representing his rocket fuel formula. The only difference was the addition of two molecules previously untested by Matthias. Now he was anxious to dive into his research again, feeling confident he finally had the elements he'd been missing in the perfection of his fuel formula.

"This was just one example," stated Rebecca. "Some of the crop circle images appear to be schematics for an anti-gravity propulsion system." Pointing to highlighted portions of the photos, she said "At a glance, these areas appear to be chambers which facilitate the manifestation of dark matter which can be generated and harvested in much the same way that solar panels convert sunlight into energy," she noted, passing the photos on to Stephan.

Once again, she watched the jaw-dropping realization of a highly acclaimed astrophysicist, as information which had eluded him for so long, was now blatantly obvious, clearly displayed in the form of crop circles!

In their rush to marginalize non-academic theories and those who presented them, mankind had all but written off clues deliberately left behind by extraterrestrial beings, who'd been attempting to communicate with us for centuries. Now, the answers were painfully obvious in their simplicity.

Turning to Heinrich, Rebecca held another image reminiscent of our solar system, depicting our sun, eight planets, and Pluto with intersecting celestial triangulation points indicating the direction from which the projectile would approach Earth.

"Hopefully, this is not to scale," stated Heinrich. "Otherwise, this projectile would be nearly the size of Idaho!"

"Kansas," stated Rebecca. "And yes... it is to scale."

Looking around the room, Rebecca could see there were no skeptics left in this group of experts, as the weight of the task before them became painfully apparent. With barely a murmur, they reviewed the copious notes, diagrams, photographs, and glyphs collected over decades of research by Adam. Somehow, it all made sense and everything in front of them pointed to solutions they'd been desperately seeking for years.

"If I'm reading this correctly," said Stephan "There seems to be one key element missing," he added, pointing to another highlighted area outside the dark matter storage chamber. "The catalyst... or some source of ignition which initiates the attraction and manifestation of dark matter inside the containment cells, and then activates it. What do you think it could be?"

"I believe I already have the catalyst, Professor Wagner," stated Rebecca. "Once you've constructed the propulsion system to the correct specifications, I'll provide you with the ignition source."

Expressing some concern, Professor Wagner said "Once the dark matter manifestation process begins within the containment cells, it's mere presence will attract additional dark matter, but without a powerful catalyst to ignite it, the dark matter will remain inert and unusable. I simply don't see how anything small enough to fit inside *this* ignition compartment could possibly be powerful enough to initiate the fusion of dark matter," concluded Professor Wagner.

"Can you build the propulsion system according to the specification indicated within the crop circles?" asked Rebecca.

Professor Wagner nodded, saying "Yes, but..."

"Then build it," interrupted Rebecca. "I will provide the ignition source," she said, meeting his gaze with a confidence that surprised everyone in the room, including herself.

"Listen, Gentlemen. I realize everyone here will have questions... big questions and important questions," stated Rebecca. "However, all the answers to each of those questions are already here, inside this room, within the great minds of the people assembled right here, right now."

Pausing for a moment, she looked around at each of them before continuing. "We do not have the luxury of time on our side, so we're going to have to cross this bridge as we're building it, and what we create here has to be launch-ready the very moment we roll it out. I'm asking you to trust me and to trust each other. Most of all, I'm asking you to trust your own abilities. That's why you're here. It's why we are all here. I just need to know whether or not I can count on you."

"I'm in," stated Professor Schultz

"I'm in, too," added Professor Wagner.

Professor Novak was next, saying "I wouldn't miss this for the world. I'm in."

Adam Levinson was the last to respond, saying "What the hell? A front row seat to what could possibly be the end of the world... I'd buy a ticket for that ride any day!"

The core of Rebecca's team was "all in". Now, they had to convince the bureaucrats holding the purse strings, that the threat was not only real, but also urgent and imminent!

As Rebecca watched the four men shaking hands and exchanging contact information, she breathed an inaudible sigh of relief, saying to herself "Thanks Mom. I love you."

Back in Kansas, Jocelyn was sitting on the couch with Brian... smiling.

CHAPTER 19

Rebecca's team of physics and engineering geniuses was truly driven, racing against a clock that exactly seven people on Earth even knew about. By her estimation, the projectile would appear in our solar system, skirting in from behind Neptune within twenty days.

Due to the non-reflective nature of the object, it would be undetectable by Earth-based radar stations, requiring Professor Doctor Heinrich Schultz to capture and recognize it visually. From that point, using available human technology, it would take approximately seven years for a vehicle launched from Earth to reach Jupiter where it could attempt to nudge the incoming projectile to within range of Jupiter's powerful gravitational field. If everything clicked perfectly into place, the object would go spiraling into the much larger planet along with any other fragments accompanying it.

With existing propulsion systems, NASA would need to launch their defensive countermeasure no later than November 15th, 2010 in order to intercept the object as it approached. They would only get one shot at it, and a thermonuclear device would require a yield of two-hundred megatons in order to redirect it into Jupiter's gravitational field.

According to available records, neither the United States nor any of the other nine countries with nuclear strike capabilities, even have such high-yield, deliverable nuclear weapons. Combine that with the non-existence of an effective delivery vehicle which could actually reach Jupiter, and our defense systems for this type of threat appear only slightly less archaic than throwing rocks at it from the moon.

The task of redirecting it would seem impossible enough for anyone outside Rebecca's team, and destroying it with a nuke was completely out of the question. During its time in the Pentagon testing facility, it was determined that a nuclear blast couldn't even scratch the olive-sized version of the object Rebecca was wearing around her neck. Pouring the same water onto an even larger duck's back would certainly not change the outcome.

Professor Doctor Matthias Novak's cutting-edge inner-atmospheric launch vehicle (affectionately referred to as the gondola) would need to lift the immense weight of the deep space delivery system into the outer atmosphere before separating and returning to Earth in a controlled descent. Once separated from the gondola, the delivery system's anti-gravitational field generator would then automatically deploy.

Just as two positively charged magnets push against each other in opposite directions, the magnetic field generated by the delivery system would be forcefully repelled by the Earth's magnetic field. Due to the immense mass differential between the two and the absence of the planet's gravitational pull as a counterbalance, the delivery vehicle would be repelled from Earth with such force, it would be cast deep into outer space at a velocity approaching the speed of light.

In deep space, the dark matter propulsion system comes online, gradually increasing the speed of the delivery vehicle and guiding the warhead to its intercept point with the incoming extraterrestrial projectile. Once visual target lock has been successfully established, the dark matter propulsion system also separates and returns to Earth, leaving the warhead free and clear, guided only by an internal gyroscope and computer-activated directional steering jets.

Due to the blistering speeds attainable using the dark matter propulsion system, once it has cleared Earth's atmosphere and magnetic field, the warhead could reach the incoming projectile in fewer than sixty minutes! This would potentially allow us to get another shot off should something in the initial calculations go awry.

With the ridiculously obvious clues laid bare in decades of documented crop circles, the entire team was highly motivated upon the realization that there was someone out there looking out for us. However, while several of these clues and modifications seemed to be powered by the same compact yet powerful energy source, Rebecca had yet to reveal that source, promising only that it would be ready the moment it was needed.

Fortunately, this obviously extraterrestrial technology was all self-sustaining. Once the devices were activated, the key would never be needed again. While each member of the team was curious and anxious to get their hands on the mystery catalyst, they understood Rebecca's reticence in revealing it. Something powerful enough to ignite the fusion process in dark matter, but stable enough to exist within the Earth's magnetic field without disrupting it, would certainly be highly coveted by the governments of every nation on Earth.

Furthermore, the potential for commercial, industrial, and military applications was mind-boggling. Even if taken alone as a starting point, the use of dark matter as a non-radioactive but inexhaustible fuel source would revolutionize the world's energy grid, allowing even the most remote locations on Earth to benefit from the availability of clean, safe energy.

Surprisingly, the experts brought in by the development team were all highly motivated, very capable professionals ranging from machinists and welders, to biochemists and engineers. They all worked very quickly, solving problems as they arose without long discussions. While only the five-person core of the team knew the entirety of what was at stake, everyone involved worked with unheard of precision and urgency. No one discussed anything outside of the team, and there were absolutely no leaks in safeguarding the information and technology applied to the project.

After three weeks of negotiating, crunching numbers, sourcing materials, and calculating the total project time and monetary expense from beginning to end, she was almost ready to make her presentation to NASA and the Department of Defense.

Suddenly, Professor Doctor Schultz came running down the stairs which led up to the massive multi-million dollar deep-space telescope in the upper level of the observatory. His eyes were as wide as flying saucers while he searched for the words his genius vocabulary simply couldn't adequately express. Finally, he settled on two words... "It's enormous!"

Everyone in the lower level of the laboratory stopped what they were doing and followed Heinrich as he rushed over to the giant plasma monitor screen, pulling up the remote recording feed from the telescope. When the image appeared, a dead silence fell over the room. For a full fifteen minutes, no one breathed a single word as they all stood mesmerized by the image before them. The projectile was just coming into view as Neptune slid out of the way continuing along its solar orbit.

The computer enhanced magnification displayed on the sixty-five-inch liquid plasma screen revealed an object so massive, it could potentially knock the Earth out of orbit were it to succeed in reaching our planet. As they all stood transfixed, staring at the planetoid sized projectile, Rebecca could sense minute vibrations pulsing through the artifact around her neck, dangling beneath her sweater.

Normally, an object of that size would have set off every "near-miss-trajectory" alarm in the northwestern hemisphere; however, looking at the deep-space detection radar monitors, the object was absolutely invisible. As everyone's eyes darted back and forth between the two screens, the importance of their work was immediately focused into brilliant clarity. The handful of experts assembled in this private Boston observatory and make-shift laboratory were staring at the adversary whose sole purpose in the galaxy was to eradicate them and completely erase even the memory of their existence. This was the enemy, and it was indeed formidable.

Looking over at Rebecca, Heinrich asked "Professor Doctor Madison, are you ready to face down this planet killer?"

Without even looking away from the monitor, she replied "No... But I will be." After a brief pause, she turned to face the entire team, adding, "We will *all* be ready."

At times, Rebecca wondered if any of them ever took breaks or left the building for more than an hour or two. As for herself, she lived, breathed, ate, slept, and existed for the purpose of presenting the case to the governmental agencies which would need to cough up the funding for this grand, bold endeavor.

Working from her home office later that evening, she calculated everything down to the last required penny. There was no pork built into her budget calculations, and the cost efficiency from start to finish on a project of this magnitude resulted in a budget that, at first glance, seemed hopelessly inadequate.

She continued late into the night, considering every potential question and every potential challenge which could arise, no matter how unlikely it might seem. Even the contractors who would provide the sourced materials needed to complete the projects, were carefully vetted, and wrestled down to their lowest possible price before she squeezed another ten percent discount out of them.

Knowing that the artifact in her possession had formerly been extensively experimented upon while at the Smithsonian Institute and the Pentagon, Rebecca requested any records they may have, using the Freedom of Information Act. While she knew they had never cracked any of the artifact's secrets, it would be helpful to her to know which tests had been performed in order to avoid unnecessary repetition.

She suspected that since the military's research had been done primarily with the potential for weaponization in mind, the artifact had simply resisted. She knew that, in order to change ownership, the artifact had to be given freely by the one in possession of it, abandoned, or obtained peacefully after the death of its previous owner. Any attempt to steal it or forcefully remove it from the present owner, even if by deception, would be met with violent resistance from the artifact. Accordingly, she theorized that trying to force information from it by subjecting it to what would amount to torture if performed on a living being, would evoke a similar response of absolute resistance.

While in Rebecca's possession, the artifact had given anything she'd asked of it. It guided her to the specific solutions encoded in geometric crop circles located all over the world, answering questions mankind had yet to even ask. Furthermore, the clues provided applied to stages of technology currently underway in her team's projects which hadn't even been developed at the time the circles were created.

Obviously, the actions of mankind were under constant scrutiny, and some outside source was providing real-time guidance in clear concise messages to her, through the artifact.

Logging out of her computer for the night, Rebecca went upstairs and showered before dragging herself to bed. Since the beginning of this project, she'd rarely slept for more than an hour or two, and even with the energizing properties of the artifact, she was looking forward to a full night's sleep for a change.

Just as she was about to fall asleep, a surprising revelation occurred to her. Suddenly, her eyes flew open and she said out loud, "Really?" Shaking her head, she asked "Am I really that slow?"

Her mind was suddenly racing! Tossing aside the covers, she quickly sprang out of bed and ran back downstairs into her office. Rifling through her desk drawers one after another, she was still shaking her head in disbelief when she finally located what she'd been looking for.

A few weeks earlier, one of her colleagues had sent her a prototype model of a wireless charging mat. It connected to her PC notebook using a bi-directional USB port which created a low-voltage magnetic field capable of charging a cellphone battery equipped with a charging receiver. Of course, being a bi-directional port, that same USB connection could also be used to transfer data from her mobile phone back to her laptop.

While she was aware that the first artifact which impacted Earth acted as a virtual homing device for the massive asteroid that followed a few million years later, it had never occurred to her that it might have been an *actual* beacon! Beacons are transmitters, and the same transmitter that sends signals, might actually be able to receive them!

After firing up and logging in to her laptop again, she attached the charging pad to one of the USB ports. With great curiosity, she removed the artifact from the deerskin pouch and placed it on the charging pad. The screen immediately went blank, leaving only a blinking white cursor on the otherwise black screen. A few seconds later, two words appeared at the cursor point.

Download complete.

CHAPTER 20

Seated at her desk in an oversized T-shirt, Rebecca stared incredulously at the message displayed in front of her.

Download Complete? What in the world had she even downloaded?

Attempting to maximize her desktop screen again, she realized that every one of the programs she'd been working on earlier had been saved and closed, including the Windows® operating system. At the very bottom of the screen was a single folder, labeled DOWNLOADS. Upon opening the folder, she discovered there were three compressed subfolders saved inside it. The first was labeled "BACKUP_files", and the other two were named "OS.exe" and "ZIP.exe".

Checking the "BACKUP_files" first, Rebecca noticed all of her data, including the operating system, had been compressed and saved within the folder. Before opening anything else, she saved that folder to an external hard drive to protect and secure her work.

Next, she clicked on the "OS.exe" file, which resulted in a message indicating "Insufficient Storage Space". Rebecca's notebook had an expanded hard drive capable of storing nearly three terabytes of data, and with the exception of the other two files in the download folder, everything else on her PC had been wiped clean.

Realizing the entire storage capacity of her computer had been converted into a glorified ZIP file, it became clear to her that she was going to need a larger computer with a lot more storage space. The expanded hard drive of her desktop PC back at the observatory, had a capacity of nearly ten terabytes, so she decided to wait until the next morning to attempt accessing the files using that computer.

Twenty minutes later, she was pulling into the parking lot at the observatory. Not surprisingly, nearly everyone else working on the project was there as well. The only person missing was Adam Levinson, who'd flown to Manchester in Southern England to photograph some newly developed crop circles.

When she walked into the laboratory wearing jeans and a NIKE® T-shirt, more than a few eyebrows were raised as she traversed the open space between the front door and her office. None of the team members had ever seen Rebecca dressed in anything other than business suits and lab-coats, and even her fellow nerds had to stop and take notice of the fact that... She was hot!

Outside her office door, she turned to face the eyes burning into her backside, saying "Drink it in boys. Five minutes from now, it'll all be yesterday's news."

No one moved when she walked into her office. A few seconds later she poked her head out the door, saying "Are you coming in, or what?"

As everyone crowded into her office, jockeying for positions where they could view the screen array on her desk, Rebecca explained that she'd received the data files from the extraterrestrial source which provided the catalyst for the dark matter propulsion system, as well as the mystery molecules for the new rocket fuel.

"What is the origin of this information... for the data **and** the catalyst?" asked Matthias.

"It originated in the same galaxy that sent us that early Christmas gift for 2012," Rebecca responded, pointing at the planetoid emerging from behind Neptune.

"Can you trust that source?" asked Stephan. "Can you be sure it will not destroy all of the work you've done thus far?"

"Well, when I downloaded it to my notebook, it backed up everything, including the operating system, before loading the new files onto my hard drive. I assume it would do the same thing here," stated Rebecca.

"Yes," said Stephan. "but this computer is linked to our entire network. All of our work could be compromised or even lost if it contains malicious software."

"On the other hand," countered Matthias "it could lead to additional positive revelations, and we need all the help we can get to stop that monster rock out there."

"So far, it's done nothing which merits suspicion," said Rebecca. "In fact, up to this point, it's provided all of the crucial elements we've used to fill in the gaps of our own research."

"I suggest we proceed and see what else it reveals," said Heinrich.

Tethering her notebook to the USB port of her desktop PC, she transferred the two files, and then clicked on the OS.exe icon. A prompt screen appeared asking "Create Backup? Y/N". Tapping the "Y" key, another prompt screen appeared which read "This Device 1/Entire Network 2".

You could actually feel the suspense in the room as everyone stared at the cursor point, blinking patiently while awaiting a decision.

"Guys...?" said Rebecca, looking around the room into the blank expressions of everyone present. "What do you think? Do we risk it taking over all of the work we've done without knowing what the outcome will be, or should we play it safe until we know more about what we're dealing with here?"

Suddenly, the phone rang. It was Adam Levinson calling from Southern England. When Rebecca answered, she told him she was putting the call on speaker so he could be included in their ongoing discussion.

"Excellent!" replied Adam. "I have something that is probably going to astonish all of you!" he said excitedly.

"Please... proceed," stated Rebecca.

"I've been set up in a vantage point overlooking a pristine barley field here for three nights now," said Adam. "Before tonight, nothing happened, then five minutes ago, three glowing orbs about the size of soccer balls descended from the cloud covering and hovered over the field. In mere seconds, it created a new crop formation right before my very eyes! It was amazing!" he ranted.

Continuing, he said "I will upload the images to my website when I get back to the hotel, but I snapped a couple of photos with my phone camera, and I'll text them to your phone now, Rebecca."

It took a few seconds, and the photo was a bit grainy, but the crop formation was easily recognizable.

"It looks sort of like a rounded check-mark to me," stated Adam. "What does it look like to you guys?" he asked.

Smiling, Rebecca passed her phone with the enlarged image around the room. One by one, every face in her office lit up after viewing the image, culminating in uncontrollable laughter infectiously spreading throughout the entire team!

"What's happening?" asked Adam, feeling as if he were being left out of some joke perpetrated at his expense.

Suppressing her own laughter, Rebecca said "Adam, you've just given us the answer to the question we've all been deliberating here!"

"Really?!" said Adam excitedly. "That's great, but you'll have to fill me in on the rest later. The orbs are active again, and I don't want to miss anything. I will call you later from the hotel once I have the high-resolution images uploaded."

Without even waiting for a response, Adam ended the call so he could concentrate on capturing the phenomenon happening in front of him.

In Rebecca's office she placed the phone on the desk beside her. Obviously, the intelligence behind the crop formations was well-aware of modern Earth culture, possibly also possessing a keen sense of humor. The image on the screen displayed a highly recognizable swoosh pattern, matching the logo adorning Rebecca's T-shirt. The only thing missing was the slogan... "Just Do It!"

The meaning behind the sudden appearance of the crop formation directly in front of one of the key team members, and his immediate need to share the image with his colleagues, who just happened to be discussing whether or not to proceed, was clearly evidence of active extraterrestrial participation.

Confidently, Rebecca tapped the number "2" on her keyboard, immediately plunging the laboratory into darkness.

As was customary in both the laboratory and the observatory above it, the overhead lights remained off, so as not to interfere with the clarity of the images being observed through the incredibly sensitive, powerful telescope. Accordingly, most of the subdued illumination came from the monitor screens of the individual workstations positioned throughout the laboratory.

As the system rebooted, every one of those stations went dark. The status message on Rebecca's screen read "Re-formatting hard drives..." followed shortly thereafter by "Installing New Operating System...". Next came "Re-configuring Local Area Network..." and "Unpacking New Files...".

After the individual workstation sequentially came back online, one final message appeared on Rebecca's monitor. "Updates Complete. Press ESC to Close Window".

After closing the window, she was taken back to her normal startup page; however, the changes to the operating system were sweeping and dramatic. Most notable, was the data compression factor. The new operating system could effectively crush big data files into micro data files, which exponentially increased the storage capacity of each individual workstation connected to the local area network. The need for this change was immediately apparent, because over a million terabytes of new data had been added to the network, distributed equitably among the various workstations as it pertained to the specific tasks being performed there.

Additionally, while all of the data at each workstation had been carefully preserved, it had also been modified to include missing formulas, revised mathematical calculations, and advanced trigonometry solutions necessary to accurately plot the course of a dark matter fueled vehicle from Earth, through the solar system, to the rendezvous point where the incoming projectile could be successfully engaged.

Just as fascinating for Professor Doctor Heinrich Schultz, was the fact that every file, every explanation, and every procedural instruction was accurately provided in over seven-thousand different languages! Furthermore, any modifications or additions made were automatically updated and shared to all related projects across the network in each of those languages!

The program was also very intuitive, in that any manual changes or updates made to one file, would automatically update any files and programs reliant upon that data, regardless of which workstation was used to input the revised information.

For instance, When Matthias's team introduced enhancements which increased the efficiency of his patented fuel burn rates, it would automatically adjust the maximum load weight of the dark matter fusion chambers and propulsion systems designed by Stephan and his team. Accordingly, when

Stephan modified the dimensions of the containment chambers by using the lighter, more heat-resistant materials recommended by the operating system, the fuel burn rate and overall vehicle efficiency were also updated for Matthias's crew and across the rest of the network.

Due to the streamlined efficiency of the data sharing process across the new network, Rebecca's financial estimates and production schedules were updated immediately and accurate to the penny. In fact, she was ready to proceed in sharing the team's findings with NASA and the Department of Defense... with one big exception.

In the massive amount of data circulated throughout the various development teams, there was one folder which only she had received. It was neither linked to, nor shared with the other integrated components of the project and required the actual placement of the artifact onto the USB charging pad in order to unlock it.

Inside the folder was a different set of schematics and engineering specifications. They were instructions describing in painstaking detail, the procedure for creation and construction of a dark matter warhead. It was so powerful that detonating it inside the Earth's atmosphere would cause a chain reaction, raising Earth's temperature to such a degree that the oceans would boil off into space.

It was the equivalent of a fail-safe option, complete with trajectory and targeting calculations which differed significantly from the data the rest of her team was using. Should the military grade nuclear warhead fail to nudge the incoming projectile into range of Jupiter's gravitational pull, and it should somehow slip through... this warhead would instantly vaporize it.

One thing was glaringly obvious. No government on Earth must ever get their hands on this information! It was truly the weapon of Rebecca's worst nightmares, and the key to it... was hanging around her neck!

CHAPTER 21

Not surprisingly, the weapon delivery system the team had designed would have broad applications across all socio-economic boundaries. It would make it possible for us to travel to other galaxies, revolutionize the Earth's energy grid, greatly advance medical technology, and somewhat equalize the playing field between Earth and extraterrestrial civilizations.

While the artifact had been on Earth for several million years, mankind was in no way, form, or fashion, ready for the knowledge which would allow them to create a dark matter energy weapon. Our civilization had yet to prove itself capable of unconditional peace across our ***own*** civilizations, ethnicities, and cultures. How would we ever be able to handle the existence of life in other galaxies, which would, without a doubt, vary dramatically from our own?

Rebecca's greatest challenge would be convincing two gigantic government organizations to accept the team's scientific findings and utilize their technology, without attempting to seize control of it and use it as a cudgel with which to threaten their perceived adversaries.

The science behind targeting the incoming projectile was staggering. It isn't like you could just point and shoot, then wait for your bullet to hit the target before popping the cork on your bottle of champagne. Every planet, asteroid, satellite, and errant piece of space debris would have to be accounted for and avoided, to say nothing of the precision calculations required to hit a moving target six-hundred-million miles away from Earth, give or take a few million miles.

Added to that, both the launch site and the target would be moving, so the point of detonation would need to be precisely timed to occur when and where the incoming projectile would be when Jupiter's gravitational pull could most easily latch onto it.

Those calculations would take an entire bank of NASA super-computers to crack, yet here, right in front of her, Rebecca had them all neatly laid out in seven-thousand languages. While she could explain that her team's developments were the result of years of research and experimentation, explaining how they even had knowledge of that big rock out there was an entirely different matter.

Attributing this to crop circles and data compiled by Adam Levinson, was certainly not going to cut it. Nevertheless, without the government's resources and equipment, reaching it in time to save the planet would be impossible.

While Rebecca puzzled over whether or not to construct the dark matter warhead, she did understand why this information had been included. The amount of red tape that went along with involving NASA and the DOD in **any** project was an invitation to scheduling delays and specification changes which could ultimately lead to them missing their window of opportunity.

Construction of the dark matter warhead would be relatively simple, requiring only the addition of a small compartment atop a separate quart-sized fusion chamber. Upon impact the compartment would open to release the catalyst into the fissile dark matter resulting in detonation. The same gondola which carries the deep space vehicle through the upper atmosphere to the outer edge of Earth's magnetic field, could also transport this warhead. In fact, being much smaller and lighter than a two-hundred-megaton nuclear warhead, it could actually reach the incoming space projectile much quicker;

however, the detonation point would need to be much more precise.

Once the dark matter inside the fusion chambers was ignited, it produced a radiant blue light which could be seen both by telescopes and the naked human eye. The dark matter which surrounds planets and stabilizes their orbits is characteristically quite different. It cannot be seen and is detected primarily by observing its effect on other celestial formations.

Detonating the warhead too close to Jupiter or any other planet would instantly draw in and ignite the surrounding dark matter which keeps their atmospheres contained and locks them into their orbital positions. That could effectively release one planet from its orbit, sending it crashing through space, potentially into the gravitational pull of another. In a worst-case scenario, the resulting planetary collisions could tear apart the entire solar system and send everything crashing into the sun.

For Rebecca, it was obvious why extraterrestrial civilizations refused to share their technology with Earth and avoided all direct contact with us. We are like babies when it comes to this stuff and there's a reason why parents keep kitchen knives out of the reach of children. If all it took to destroy the solar system was a quart of energized dark matter and the rock around her neck, there was certainly no way in hell, Rebecca was going to let this technology fall into the hands of anyone else.

As she sat in her office considering the pitch she was about to make to the government, her mobile phone rang. It was Adam again.

"Hello, Adam," she said, happy for the interruption. "Welcome back to the USA!"

"It's good to be back, Professor, and I brought some amazing photographs and video footage for you and the team," said Adam.

"Great!" Replied Rebecca. "I can't wait to see them!"

"Hey, what are you doing right now?" asked Adam.

"Just sitting here going over the notes for my presentation to the peanut gallery," answered Rebecca.

"When was the last time you had dinner that didn't come out of the freezer or a can?" Adam asked, curiously.

The silence on the other end of the line was telling...

"Okay, throw on something other than a lab coat, and meet me at *The Barking Crab*, say... in one hour," said Adam. "I'm buying."

Before she could object, the call ended.

Rebecca's social life consisted of chance meetings with total strangers at gas stations, drive-thru restaurant windows, and in the canned goods aisle at the local supermarket. All of her colleagues were nerds just like her, and their conversations eventually devolved into shop talk which was no different than being at work all day.

Still, Adam's call had given her an excuse to take a much-needed mental break from the project and clear her head. Besides, he was right. She hadn't dressed up for dinner since the night she was awarded the Nobel Prize, and that seemed like it was a lifetime ago.

Adam was pleasantly surprised when she walked into the restaurant, first of all, because she was actually on time and secondly, because she looked absolutely amazing.

Wearing a dark grey knee-length skirt, the tulip-cut accentuated her slender but attractive figure. Her white silk blouse was tucked into the skirt and the two were cinched together at her waistline by a wide black belt bearing a silver buckle which resembled an artistic rendering of Saturn tilted at a slight angle. Two-inch black patent-leather pumps rounded off the look as she walked toward the table where Adam was standing to welcome her as she approached.

Reaching out to shake his extended hand, she said "If you say one word about me looking weird in this outfit, I will lose every ounce of courage it took for me to put it on, and I'll run straight out the door again."

"Actually, you look beautiful," said Adam, pulling out a chair for her. "Please... have a seat."

Over or d'oeuvres, Alan explained how he'd interviewed a number of people who'd been tracking and cataloging crop formations for decades. They were able to provide him with additional, previously undocumented images and eye-witness accounts of the crop circles as they were being created.

Furthermore, most of them were of the mindset that this phenomenon was occurring in order to facilitate contact between mankind and extraterrestrial entities. They also believed that these formations may be intended as a warning to Earth, regarding some impending cataclysm.

Rebecca also explained what they'd been working on during his call from England, and how its timing was the deciding factor which encouraged them to install the new operating system. Now that their individual pockets of knowledge had been fused into one cohesive database, the network seemed more like a living entity, intelligently sharing information to each team member according to their specific needs, greatly accelerating the pace and accuracy of their work.

"When is your meeting with NASA and the DOD?" asked Adam.

"The day after tomorrow," answered Rebecca. "I'm actually very well prepared for it, but at the same time, I'm about to be the bearer of the worst news mankind has ever had to digest, while simultaneously offering them the only viable solution for solving the crisis."

"You didn't create the problem, Rebecca," said Adam. "In fact, without your involvement, it would have taken years for them to even discover the damn thing flying straight at us!"

"People would go on living their lives, falling in love, and creating families, happy in their ignorance until Santa arrived three days early, with the present no one asked for," said Rebecca, staring blankly into her wine glass.

"Ignorance is bliss," replied Adam. "...until you realize it could have been stopped if only someone had spoken up in time. You, my dear Professor, are that someone."

"Hopefully, they won't decide to shoot the messenger," said Rebecca.

"If they do, they may as well save the next bullet for themselves, because they'll be sealing the fates of over seven-billion souls who don't stand a chance without you," Adam responded, raising his glass to toast her as the waiter arrived with their food.

As nervous as she'd been when she walked in, she was surprisingly comfortable having dinner with Adam. Unlike her students at the University or the other team members she'd been working with, Adam had a worldly air about him that made her feel like an adult. He could listen objectively as she expressed her ideas yet also express his own differing opinions without criticizing her.

Despite the fact that he wasn't an academic scholar, his skill in the field of investigative research had earned him a coveted Pulitzer Prize for Public Service Journalism. He was extremely intelligent, which came across quite clearly in his eloquent manner of speaking, yet she never felt as if he was patronizing toward her.

It was a shock to both of them when their waiter approached, saying the restaurant would be closing soon. Looking around, they discovered they were the last remaining guests. After settling their tab, they wandered out into the parking lot, both instinctively looking up into the stars.

"Do you think anyone else even realizes how little time we may have left?" asked Adam.

"I hope not," replied Rebecca. "How could they ever look into the stars again with wonder and amazement in their eyes if they did?"

"Well," said Adam. "Fortunately, not everything wonderful and amazing is a hundred light years away."

As she lowered her gaze from the heavens and looked over at him, he was watching her.

Breaking the nervous silence, Rebecca asked, "Can I give you a lift back to your hotel?"

"That would be great," answered Adam with a nod.

His hotel wasn't far from the restaurant, and within five minutes, they were pulling into the roundabout and up to the front entrance.

"Thank you for the ride, Rebecca... and thank you for having dinner with me tonight," said Adam.

"Don't mention it," said Rebecca. "It was wonderful."

As he exited the car, he leaned down and looked in through the lowered passenger window saying, "One day, before the world ends, promise me I'll get to kiss you goodnight."

Feeling oddly relaxed there beneath the hotel overhang, Rebecca said "I'll think about it. After all, worst case scenario, we still have ten years... right?"

"Right," said Adam with a smile, waving as he turned and walked through the doors into the hotel lobby.

Once in his suite, he kicked off his shoes taking a seat in the living room, crossing his legs, and putting his feet up on the ottoman. Leaning back in the chair, he looked up at the ceiling, replaying the delightful evening he'd just spent with Rebecca.

A few seconds later, there was a soft knock at the door, snapping him out of his reverie. Remembering the express courier parcel, he requested his editor have sent to this address, he opened the door expecting to find the concierge. To his utter surprise, it was Rebecca.

"I've decided ten years would be a bit too long," she said, pushing him into the room, and kicking the door closed behind them.

CHAPTER 22

During the short flight from Boston to Washington DC, Rebecca stared blankly out the window. She'd received her Nobel Prize in physics for her work in the field of time compression and utilization of the perception differential. However, as the youngest Nobel Lauriat in the History of that coveted prize, it was at times difficult to convince others of her intelligence and of her ability to address and solve big problems.

While she was confident in her knowledge and preparations, she was still a twenty-four-year-old kid in the minds of many of her contemporaries, and she would need to overcome that hurdle immediately in order to convince those who would be seated across the table from her in a Pentagon conference room.

She was barely on the ground at Ronald Reagan Washington National Airport when she received a text from the driver who would meet her at the terminal gate. Since she'd only be in Washington DC for one night, she hadn't checked any luggage and proceeded directly to the gate where the driver met and escorted her to a waiting limousine. Within minutes, she was being signed in at the Pentagon.

As always, Rebecca was notoriously early. Still, when she arrived, the room was already filled with enough brass to set off metal detectors, and everything she'd asked for was in place, ready for her presentation.

The last to arrive was the Director of NASA who barged into the room precisely thirty seconds before the scheduled meeting time. Without exchanging pleasantries of any kind, he said "Good evening, Miss Madison," with apparent disinterest. "You've got twenty minutes... Go!"

Rebecca replied, "It's Professor Doctor Madison, and I only need ten."

The room went silent. After a few seconds, the Director said "Very well, Professor Doctor Madison. Please proceed."

Standing, Rebecca lowered the lights and began her presentation. "Twenty days ago, an object entered our solar system, sneaking in behind Neptune. It is on a direct collision course with Earth and will enter our atmosphere, impacting the planet on December 21st, 2012. It will kill everyone."

Looking down at her watch, she added. "Wow! Now, what am I supposed to do with the remaining nine minutes?"

As she brought the lights back up and began packing the presentation materials back into her briefcase, the buzz in the conference room grew into a loud murmur before evolving into a boisterous frenzied discussion among the meeting attendees.

"Quiet please!" said the Director loudly, before finally shouting, "Everyone... Shut the hell up!" while pounding his fist on the conference room table.

The buzz in the room subsided as the Director turned toward Rebecca saying, "Professor Doctor Madison, please forgive me for my dismissive attitude earlier. You've obviously put a lot of thought into this, and you deserve to be heard out. I'm sorry. Please continue."

"Thank you, Mr. Director," she said, once again removing a manila envelope from her briefcase. Walking around the conference table, she placed a copy of her presentation on the leather blotters in front of each attendee.

"The object headed toward Earth originated outside our solar system, and possibly even outside our galaxy," she continued. "It has a total area of eighty-two thousand square miles, or two-hundred-thirteen-thousand kilometers. Its molecular structure makes it invisible to Earth based deep space radar detection systems, and impervious to all of our conventional, focused beam, and atomic energy weapons systems. At its current velocity, it will reach and destroy Earth on December 21st, 2012."

"In order to stop it with existing weapons and technology," Rebecca continued, "we would need to launch a two-hundred-megaton nuclear warhead no later than eight years from now, which would travel for approximately twenty-six months, to intercept the object as it approaches Jupiter. If positioned properly, the blast will divert the object into range of Jupiter's gravitational field, effectively sucking it into a much larger planet where the impact could be absorbed without the danger of a cataclysm."

"Once again, using current technology and weapons systems, we would only get one shot at this. If we miss, or employ our countermeasures too late, the projectile will pass by Jupiter with nothing between it and Earth that can stop it."

Looking around the room, she had everyone's full attention as she continued. "For the past year, I have been working with a team of top physicists, astrophysicists, engineers, chemists, and experts on extraterrestrial intelligence, to develop a plan of action which could possibly be our last hope for preventing the total and complete annihilation of the planet. This team has developed new proprietary technologies and propulsion systems which could significantly lower the intercept time, dramatically improving our chances of success. Working together with NASA, the Department of Defense, and a number of private civilian companies and organizations, my team could implement a plan which significantly improves our chances of survival, but we must act quickly. There is absolutely zero room for excessive bureaucracy, and there's no pork built into our funding calculations."

The beeping sound coming from Rebecca's watch alerted her that it was time for the next element of her presentation.

Speaking into the video conference camera, she said "Professor Doctor Heinrich Schultz, are you ready to introduce these gentlemen to our discovery?"

"Yes, Professor Doctor Madison," replied Heinrich.

Turning to face the room, Rebecca said, "Gentlemen, I present to you... Deep Space Object Santa-2012"

The image appearing on the monitor showed the massive object complete with live tracking data and computer-generated graphic depictions showing its size, shape, density, velocity, estimated weight, and the time and date of impact with Earth, barring prior intervention. It also showed countdown clocks for effective countermeasure deployment, and time to intercept within Jupiter's gravitational field.

With the image on the monitors effectively sucking all the oxygen from the room, Rebecca concluded her presentation saying, "At this time, I'd be happy to entertain any questions. Please be brief, because the Director is short on time, and I'd hate to keep him from focusing on more pressing issues."

At that point, the Director told his aide, "Cancel all of my remaining meetings for this evening, and get the President on the phone... Now!" As the aide scurried toward the door, he added "Tell Rachel to send someone in from catering, because we are all going to be here for a while tonight."

As predicted, the questions came flying in like an asteroid shower over an empty desert sky. Her entire team joined the discussion via teleconference, answering questions regarding the ground-breaking fuel formula and inner atmospheric delivery system developed by Professor Doctor Matthias Novak, as well as the magnetic field and outer atmospheric dark matter propulsion systems developed by Professor Doctor Stephan Wagner.

Even those who had nearly vilified Adam Levinson for his outlandish theories and crop circle interpretations, had to acknowledge the clarity of the data he produced leading to the discovery of the object which, as he had correctly predicted, would enter our solar system from behind Neptune.

Due to the urgency of the situation, it was obvious we would need a unified team of experts assembled from countries all over the world in order to confront this existential threat. Fortunately, the critical areas of cooperation were already provided in every language used on the planet, and the universal operating system shared by Rebecca's team made integration of new information seamless, without compromising the intellectual ownership of proprietary information, regardless of where it originated. Since everything was explained in remarkably simple and concise language, each process requiring multi-lateral cooperation could be easily understood and acted upon.

When NASA officials combed through Rebecca's financial calculations for the project, they were astounded by the frugality exercised in compiling the numbers. She was correct in her assertion that there was no pork built into the proposed budget. In fact, she had secured pricing that the Department of Defense had never been able to wrangle from its suppliers, and even though they were now involved in the process, the contractors stuck to the pricing Professor Doctor Madison had worked out for them, which resulted in billions of dollars in savings when compared to the best prices obtained by negotiators for NASA and the DOD.

While there were questions pertaining to the catalyst which would bring all of this new technology to life, Rebecca held that trump card close to the vest (literally), explaining that it would be available when the first of the dark matter fusion chambers was completed and ready for ignition. Once one of them was activated, it could be used to attract and initiate the fusion process in the remaining chambers without ever again requiring the original catalyst. Afterwards, each subsequent fusion chamber could be used as a non-depletable, safe energy source, comparable to lighting a candle by using another candle, except these candles would never burn out.

Rebecca's planned trip had ballooned into a three-day excursion; however, both NASA and the DOD were willing to accept all conditions set forth by her team, offering them unprecedented cooperation and autonomy on the project as long as there were no perceived threats to our national security interests. With the greatest minds in the entire world coming together to prevent this looming disaster, scientists had never been more unified or willing to share their advanced technologies as they were now, in service of this common cause.

Unfortunately, there aren't only scientists in the world, and with the necessity of involving others in the grand scheme of things, came the increased potential for information leaks and the surreptitious greed of those looking to line their pockets by profiting from this potential worldwide apocalypse.

After the extended trip, Rebecca was looking forward to sleeping in her own bed again. She was so exhausted, she missed things she'd have otherwise spotted immediately. Bumping into the same person in two different airports within a three-hour time period would normally have set off alert signals in her mind. However, due to her physical exhaustion and mental fatigue, her guard was down when she headed out to the long-term parking lot at Logan International.

She had no idea she was being followed as she made her way to her vehicle which she had purposely parked at the back of the lot in a location less likely to be dinged by other drivers. Her guard was down. The artifact's... was not.

When the two men surveilling her approached, closing in on her from each side, the artifact violently intervened. Emitting an intense auditory burst along the radio band being used for their in-ear communication devices, both of their brains immediately began to hemorrhage, causing blood to pour from their ears, eyes, and nostrils as they crumbled to the garage floor in excruciating pain! Reacting to their screams, Rebecca rushed toward the man closest to her while reaching in her purse for her phone to dial 9-1-1. By the time she reached him, his convulsions had stopped just as his heart had. Dashing over to the other man, she discovered he had suffered a similar agonizing fate. By the time security and the paramedics arrived in the parking lot, there was nothing else anyone could do.

Rebecca gave her statement to the responding security officers before being escorted back out to her vehicle in the long-term parking lot. When she finally made it back to her condo, she fell into bed exhausted, sleeping through the night without interruption.

It was so good to be home.

CHAPTER 23

Rebecca awoke to the insistent pounding at her door and intermittent, ringing of her doorbell. The sun was already shining brightly through her bedroom window when she opened her eyes, disoriented after being snatched from deep sleep.

Slipping into the bathrobe she'd tossed across the armchair the night before, she headed down the stairs to the front door and peered curiously through the peephole. It was Adam, flanked by three uniformed officers.

Quickly opening the door, she asked "Adam, what's going on?"

Breathing an obvious sigh of relief, he put his arms around her hugging her close to him. "Thank God!" he said. "We thought they'd gotten to you!"

"You thought **who** had gotten to me?" asked Rebecca. "Why are the police here with you?"

"Just get dressed, and I'll explain everything on the way," Adam answered.

"On the way to where?" she asked. "Adam, what's going on?"

Looking at the officers flanking him on the left and right, he said "Rebecca, those men you reported in the parking garage last night... they were professionals. They were trying to abduct you."

"What!?" she asked incredulously. "Why would someone want to abduct me?"

Following her inside, he said "Listen, I'll explain while you get dressed, but hurry, okay?"

Nodding, Rebecca rushed up the stairs to her bedroom with Adam close behind her. As she dressed, he told her "The two men you found in the parking garage last night were armed, and both of them had the same photo of you, taken at the airport in DC."

"What!?" exclaimed Rebecca. "What do they want with me?"

"Sweetheart, after your presentation at the Pentagon on Tuesday, you have become the most important person on the planet. If someone were to take you, the ransom they could demand for your safe return would be astronomical. You are the lynchpin for this entire project, which makes you invaluable to Earth's survival."

"Oh my God!" exclaimed Rebecca. "The man who bumped into me at the DC airport, then again at Logan International last night..."

"Which man?" asked Adam. "Was it one of the men from the parking garage?"

"No. It was a different person," Rebecca answered.

"Tall, brown hair, wearing an orange ballcap?" Adam asked.

"Yes!" Exclaimed Rebecca. "He also had a short stubbly beard."

"They found him too," said Adam. "He was inside a delivery van, parked near a service elevator in the basement. The motor was still running, but he was in pretty much the same condition as the other two."

"What the hell!?" said Rebecca. "What happened to all of them?"

"All of them were wearing the same in-ear communication devices, and apparently some kind of cross-interference caused them all to malfunction," Adam explained.

"Now, what were you wearing last night when the guy with the ballcap bumped into you?"

"All that stuff," said Rebecca, pointing to the garments on the floor near her bedroom closet.

Collecting her clothing from the floor, he wrapped everything into a bundle and tucked it under his arm before ushering Rebecca out the door to the officers waiting outside. Surrounding her on all sides, they escorted both Rebecca and Adam to what appeared to be a Black Secret Service issue Chevy Suburban.

Inside, Adam handed Rebecca's clothes to an agent seated behind them. Using a scanner, he quickly discovered the electronic bug attached to the hemline of her suit jacket and removed it, dropping it into a reflective lead-lined envelope.

Heading toward the observatory perched atop Bellevue Hill, they were confronted with a barricade erected to control access into and out of the compound. When they reached the laboratory, they discovered it was swarming with armed military personnel.

"What the hell is going on here!?" asked Rebecca. "Why are all of these people here?"

When the vehicle stopped, a man approached and opened the door for them, saying "Good morning Professor Doctor Madison," then nodded toward Adam, adding "Mister Levinson."

Continuing, he said "I'm Agent Knight, and I do apologize for the massive intrusion, but effective immediately, you and your entire team are under Secret Service protection as ordered by the President of the United States."

When Rebecca looked over at Adam, he said "That's what I've been trying to tell you, Rebecca. Somehow, your name was leaked out of that meeting at the Pentagon, and now you are the most important, most sought after person walking this planet."

"I'm sure you understand the urgency of our situation, Professor Doctor Madison," said Agent Knight. "Without your team, Earth has exactly one snowball's chance in hell at surviving this worldwide crisis."

Looking at Agent Knight, Rebecca said "Both NASA and the DOD assured me, we'd have complete autonomy in this project. This doesn't feel like complete autonomy to me."

"I understand," said Agent Knight. "but I assure you. We are only here to provide a secure working environment for you and your team. No one will interfere with your work, and if there is anything you need, and I do mean **anything**, I personally guarantee you'll get it as quickly as humanly possible."

Continuing, Agent Knight added, "Professor Doctor Schultz has been gracious enough to let us set up temporary living quarters for everyone in your team, and we'll do everything possible to ensure your privacy isn't infringed upon."

"Oh, what the hell..." said Rebecca, looking around the laboratory. "We all spend most of our lives here anyway. We might as well make it official."

Before disappearing into her office, Rebecca looked back to say "Agent Knight, can you have someone bring some of my clothes and other essentials from my house? I just spent three days at the Pentagon wearing the same outfit, and I do not intend to continue that streak for even one more day." Hesitating, she added "Oh, and make sure it's a female agent. Guys apparently have no idea what a woman considers 'essential'."

"Of course," replied Agent Knight. "I'll send someone out for them right away."

For the remainder of the day and deep into the evening, Rebecca and her team worked tirelessly with scientists from around the world to connect all of the dots necessary in putting this gargantuan puzzle together as quickly as possible.

As promised, Agent Knight and his small army of security agents were nearly invisible inside the laboratory and knowing that no one had to leave the premises to go eat, shower, sleep, or change clothes, the team's productivity actually increased substantially. Of course, the new operating system tracked and updated everything as the project progressed, so while unauthorized individuals were prevented from entering the facility, useful information from all over the world flowed freely into and out of the project headquarters there in Professor Doctor Schultz's observatory.

With all possible distractions eliminated, it was easy to get large pieces of the project completed, even though time seemed to evaporate for those immersed in their individual tasks. It was shortly after midnight when Rebecca heard the knock on her office door.

Looking over her right shoulder, she noticed Adam standing in the doorway smiling as he watched her.

"You know what?" said Adam. "I think you **are** the catalyst."

"Really?" said Rebecca. "Just what makes you think that?"

"First of all, you are the engine powering this entire project. Next, you never seem to run out of energy even though you work twenty hours a day, and finally," Adam added "you have this beautiful glow about you when you're working at optimal efficiency."

"And just how long have you been watching me?" asked Rebecca as a sly smile formed at the corners of her lips.

"Honestly... It was in Oslo when you got your Nobel. I couldn't take my eyes off you. After shadowing you and following your research for months, I was already impressed. Even before I interviewed you, I knew you were going to be selected," Adam explained.

"That night at the awards banquet, when you walked up to the stage to give your acceptance speech, I finally understood your theory of time compression and the perception differential, because everything slowed to a crawl around me. It was as if I could have lived my entire life with you in the space of a single footstep."

As she smiled at him, Adam continued. "In my mind, I could see you walking over to me and it was as if everything around us had simply stopped. You were so gorgeous standing there in that slinky black full-length dress. For a moment, I could actually feel your hand against my face, and as impossible as it may have seemed, you said..."

"You are a beautiful, beautiful man," Rebecca said, finishing the sentence Adam had begun. "And then I tiptoed and kissed you, and you wrapped your arms around my waist."

"Yes..." Adam said very slowly, obviously perplexed. "How did you know...?"

"What good is a physics theory that remains unproven?" said Rebecca.

"You really did kiss me that night, didn't you?" Adam stated, with the most adorably quizzical look on his face.

Turning off her monitors, Rebecca stood up and slowly walked over to Adam, pressing herself against him in the frame of her office door. Looking up into his eyes, she said "I'd have fucked you right then and there, had I believed I could've gotten away with it."

Backing away from him, she left the office and walked down the hallway towards their temporary living accommodations. After a few steps, she turned to look back at Adam.

"Are you coming?" she asked.

Looking around the laboratory to confirm that time hadn't actually stopped again, he could see everyone else was still diligently working on their independent projects, in real time, with the efficiency of a beehive. When he turned his attention back to Rebecca, she was slowly backing into the darkness of the long hallway.

From the shadows, he heard her say "I'm not even going to try to hide this from everyone else for the next eight years, so you might as well get comfortable with your new normal."

Smiling, and shaking his head in amazement, Adam followed her voice into the darkness.

CHAPTER 24

While the sequestered team worked diligently on optimizing Professor Doctor Novak's inner atmospheric delivery system and the dark matter containment cells for Professor Doctor Stephan Wagner's deep space propulsion system, the design specifications were shared seamlessly and in real-time with the engineering and construction teams at NASA and the DOD. Because much of the available technology within the government agencies could be repurposed to accommodate Matthias's new engines and fuel system requirements, NASA was able to begin the simultaneous construction of not one, but two gondolas.

Although the dark matter containment cells for the deep space propulsion system were relatively simple to design and construct, the electronic fail-safe modules mandated by the DOD were a bit trickier to integrate. Since the modules were one-hundred percent redundant in the first place, it was primarily a safeguard to give NASA the feeling they'd actually contributed something to the project.

In reality, the fusion process which occurs inside the containment cells would be rendered inert once exposed to the Earth's inner atmosphere and magnetic field. The containment cells themselves, were actually equipped with rudimentary magnetic field generators which allowed the fusion process to occur inside the cells. Should the cell integrity become compromised allowing the activated dark matter to escape, it would immediately become inert, harmlessly reintegrating with the invisible dark matter abundantly present inside Earth's atmosphere.

Frankly, the unknown range of uses for someone able to harness the energy of active dark matter, genuinely terrified military analysts inside the DOD. While their mandated safety feature was well-intended, there was only one object on the entire planet capable of igniting active dark matter inside Earth's atmosphere, and there was no way anyone, except for Professor Doctor Madison was ever getting their hands on it.

The first of the dark matter containment cells was constructed completely inside the laboratory. It was only the size of a small soup can; however, once activated it would serve as the match capable of initiating the fusion process inside every future containment cell which followed through infinity.

While the only danger associated with the initial activation process would require Rebecca's intentional unification of the artifact with the active dark matter inside the containment cell, without it being rendered inert by Earth's inner atmosphere, she cleared the entire facility of all personnel prior to lighting the match.

Inside her office, there were no monitoring devices of any kind and no one present to witness the initial ignition procedure. The same USB charging pad used to instantly download a million terabytes of information, was plugged into a similar port built into the match. Upon placing the artifact atop the pad, the deep bluish-gray stone immediately began to glow, turning bright gold as it seemed to be drawing energy from the surrounding atmosphere!

Once the glow of the artifact stabilized into a steady pulse, Rebecca pushed and held the ignition button atop the match, immediately igniting the dark matter inside the containment cell. The fusion process rapidly transformed the invisible dark matter into a beautifully glowing blue lantern.

Carefully placing her hand against the match, she discovered it was not only cool... it was actually cooler than the air surrounding it. Picking it up, she held it up in front of her saying, "And God said... 'Let there be light'."

After allowing herself a few minutes to marvel at the planet's new source of abundant, clean, safe energy, she sent a group text to her amazing team waiting outside beyond the security perimeter. Even from her office inside the laboratory, she could hear them cheering at the achievement of their first physical milestone following months of unprecedented cooperation among the world's most brilliant minds from nearly every country on Earth.

After placing the artifact inside the pouch dangling from her neck and concealing it beneath her blouse and lab coat again, she unlocked the front door and opened it for the cheering crowd of geniuses waiting outside.

As they all poured back into the building, there was an excitement among the team which was nearly tangible as they gathered around their beautifully glowing blue match. Over the next few days that followed, they conducted a myriad of tests and measurements to confirm the stability and accuracy of the energy generated by the device, before using it to activate two similar devices; one of which, was installed and used to power the entire facility, completely removing it from the city's power grid.

The other match was transported to Hanscom Air Force Base in the dark of night using an unmarked van surrounded by a veritable caravan of security vehicles and personnel. It reached Andrews Air Base without incident where it was once again, transported to NASA Headquarters in a nondescript security convoy.

Even the formerly arrogant Director of NASA was delighted upon receiving news of the device's arrival, and immediately made his way back to NASA Headquarters. His first call was to the President, followed by a second congratulatory call to Professor Doctor Rebecca Madison in her office at the laboratory in Boston.

The team in Washington DC quickly confirmed that the energy generated by their device was identical to that of the two devices in the Boston facility. Within two days, they were outfitting the twin deep space delivery vehicles with the new dark matter propulsion system.

Had it been up to Rebecca's team, they would have been prepared to conduct a test launch of the defensive countermeasure within three years; however, due to the involvement of actual nuclear weapons technology, the DOD's slow, deliberative pace, while remaining well within the parameters of the deployment window, still slowed things to a crawl.

For the countermeasure to be effective, it would require a warhead capable of delivering a two-hundred megaton punch, which was something none of the world's nuclear powers were even in possession of. While the United States and Russia were busy posturing and making excuses as to why neither of them actually had the weapon, both countries had been bragging about during saber-rattling sessions over the previous decade, the solution came, quite unexpectedly, from another country... North Korea!

While the North Korean military had absolutely no way of delivering the massive warhead due to their lacking missile technology, they did have the actual warhead ready, hoping to one day be capable of delivering a "knock-out-punch" with a single projectile at some undeterminable point in the future.

Realizing that without sufficient energy to generate the required blast wave, the incoming planetoid would be the only thing delivering a punch of any kind in the near future. In light of that undeniable inevitability, and due to the fact that they were decades away from possessing the required launch technology, the Koreans offered up the device as their country's contribution to preservation of the Human race.

After providing the weapon's precise size, weight, and mass specifications, a proportionate mock-up of the device could be constructed, and launch testing could proceed. While the actual weapon was transported in a multi-national naval armada escorted by military regiments and high-level diplomats representing each of the ten nuclear nations, the engineering team in Cape Canaveral got to work mounting the dud device for their first series of launch tests.

The first tests were simply to measure the thrust and burn rates created by the new rocket and fuel assemblies for the gondola. Every stage of the inner-atmospheric transport system testing was successful, resulting in telemetry results which precisely mirrored those calculated by the new operating system. Furthermore, the gondola separation test and computer guided return flight was executed without even a centimeter of deviation at the landing site.

The next test launch incorporated the first and second phases of the deep space delivery system. After separation from the gondola, the magnetic field propulsion generator deployed precisely as predicted at the cusp of the Earth's magnetic field. The resulting acceleration of the vehicle occurred so quickly, were it not for the pre-positioned satellite surveillance system, it would have been impossible to track.

Four point six seconds later, the dark matter fusion drive came online, pushing the deep space delivery vehicle up to, then beyond the speed of light, as the magnetic field surrounding the vehicle acted as a powerful shield against any manner of space debris it could possibly encounter. After only fifty-one minutes, it approached Jupiter, where the dark matter propulsion drive separated from the warhead, firing retro-boosters as it disengaged.

With the fake warhead free and clear, the navigation jets guided it precisely to the pre-programmed detonation point, while the transport vehicle dipped down, navigating toward the outer edge of Jupiter's magnetic field disappearing behind the massive planet. Precisely eleven point six seconds later, it reappeared on the opposite side of the planet at the edge of Jupiter's gravitational field. When it reached the trajectory coordinates which would bring it back towards Earth, the magnetic field generator came back online, activating at the outer edge of Jupiter's magnetic field.

Due to the planet's massive size, and a magnetic field ten times stronger than Earth's, the acceleration of the delivery vehicle as it was repelled from Jupiter's orbit was even faster, reaching a velocity of nearly two times the speed of light before the dark matter propulsion system came back online three seconds later. For the next forty-four minutes, the dark matter fusion drive pushed the transport vehicle back towards home before extinguishing and firing retro-boost engines to slow the vehicle as it approached Earth's orbit.

By modulating the polarity of the magnetic field generator, it cushioned the impact of the vehicle as it pushed up against Earth's magnetic field, this time, slowing the vehicle without repelling it back out into space. Decelerating as it passed through the ionosphere the vehicle exited the friction belt in a controlled glide as it returned to the designated landing pad, touching down... dead center!

In control rooms across the planet, screams of jubilation filled the air, as Earth's champion came to rest, and the engines shut down after a blindingly successful test run.

In Boston, Rebecca turned to face Professor Doctor Heinrich Schultz with a smile that stretched from ear to ear, saying, "Now... Now we're ready!"

CHAPTER 25

After the flawless performance of the countermeasure delivery system, one would believe the world could finally come together and coalesce around an unprecedented era of cooperation. One would also be dead wrong.

With the countdown clock showing just under one year remaining before launch, deep-seated rivalries once again began to appear between Russia, the United States, China, and North Korea. With a tested countermeasure in place, they began contemplating the shifting power balance which placed the United States, as the originating country, clearly at the top of the pyramid.

Despite ongoing real-time telemetry tracking the exact position of the incoming projectile, and the plethora of data verifying and re-verifying the precise detonation point for the warhead, there were disagreements as to whether or not nudging the planet into Jupiter as opposed to destroying it, would be the most effective plan of action.

The North Koreans seemed to prefer a head-on collision and detonation, confident of the lethality of their mega-warhead. It was obvious to the Americans that North Korea simply wanted to use the event as propaganda to demonstrate the power of the weapon they'd created, earning them legitimate claim to a front row seat on the world's nuclear stage.

On the other hand, China and Russia were more interested in gaining control of the technology behind the catalyst capable of initiating the dark matter fusion process. While they never took an official position on that particular matter in the world's joint press releases, those working within the diplomatic circles involved in the project were cognizant of their indirect assertions that the catalyst should also be shared as part of the worldwide dark matter energy program.

Despite the obvious fact that any active dark matter containment cell could be used to ignite an infinite number of additional power cells, they felt this key element of the energy chain shouldn't be exclusive to any one country in particular.

Even after multiple assurances from the United States that the science behind the catalyst was proprietary information, and no longer necessary in the production of unlimited, clean, safe energy, friction began to develop over that specific element of the joint defense project.

The closer the launch date loomed, the more dug-in each side became, until China and Russia threatened to sabotage the joint accord by pressing North Korea to demand the return of their massive nuclear warhead. Once again, supposed statesmen were signaling they'd rather see the world end, than find a compromise.

Even as diplomats and politicians jockeyed for position and soundbites on the evening news, the analysts, physicists, engineers, architects, astronomers, and astrophysicists actually working to solve the problem, continued without regard to what was happening in parliamentary and congressional chambers. The groundbreaking science developed and applied to this project was actually benefitting mankind in a myriad of substantial areas.

The Norwegian team discovered that by exposing unfiltered or contaminated water to blue light emitted by the dark matter fusion cells, it could be completely purified and reduced to its basic form of H_2O removing all contaminants which weren't a part of water's basic molecular structure, within seconds. The same science could also be applied to medical procedures requiring absolutely sterile environments.

At Stanford University Medical Center, the magnetic micro-filter element developed for the gondola's fuel combustion system proved highly effective in filtering out cancer cells from human blood, dramatically improving the survival rates for leukemia patients.

Worldwide integration of the dark matter energy cells, had already begun to reduce the planet's overall carbon footprint, actually decreasing the average global temperature by nearly two degrees in only four years.

One week before deploying Earth's global countermeasure, North Korea refused to release the activation code for their nuclear warhead. Claiming that the United States was seeking to undermine the North Korean regime by forcing unilateral disarmament of their nuclear weapons arsenal, they found immediate backing from Russia and China, and demanded release of the technology pertaining to the dark matter fusion catalyst.

As Rebecca's team was busy with their final preparations, updating telemetry data and plotting the precise course of the countermeasure delivery system, and fueling both of the inner atmospheric transport vehicles, she and Adam were puzzling over what sort of unexpected last-minute adjustments would inevitably rear their ugly heads. They didn't have to wait very long, because a moment later, Agent Knight knocked on her office door.

"Good afternoon, Agent Knight," said Rebecca.

"Good afternoon, Professor Doctor Madison," he answered in a tone that was absolutely flat. Standing behind him were three agents wearing government issued black suits and reflective sunglasses.

"What's wrong, Agent Knight?" asked Rebecca. He'd only rarely been inside the laboratory or observatory, and he'd never been in the company of other agents. "Why the additional backup today?"

"We need to escort you to Washington DC, Ma'am," answered Agent Knight. "Something urgent has come up and you are the only one who can provide the necessary guidance. The Director of NASA has called a meeting of the diplomats representing the International Response Task Force, and we need to bring clarity to the matter as quickly as possible. Hopefully, we'll have you home in time for the evening news," he added.

Turning to face Adam, Rebecca said "Duty calls, Sweetheart." Tiptoeing to kiss him, she added "Keep everything together for me, and don't go saving the world or anything before I get back!"

"I wouldn't think of it," said Adam. "That, my dear, is your job."

During the nearly eight years of working with NASA and the DOD, there had been several of these unplanned meetings. They were usually called to give politicians and diplomats facetime with Professor Doctor Madison, rarely (if ever) resulting in deviations from the plan as she'd initially presented it.

As he watched her leaving the office with the Agents, he suddenly realized she was the only one actually moving, and she was headed back toward him!

"This stinks to high heaven, Babe," she said to him as they conversed inside their private time bubble. "These guys are after the catalyst and there's no way in hell I'm giving it to them."

"Well, what's your play?" asked Adam.

"I installed a decoy which will take them awhile to figure out, but I'll need your help." Taking his hand, she led him over to her desktop computer, saying "I will have them initiate a video call to you, here in my office. When I say so, I need you to press

CONTROL, ALT, BACKSPACE, and the backslash key simultaneously, and hold them until the seventeen-digit code appears."

"That's all?" asked Adam.

"Yes. It's only a random code of nonsense, but it will keep them occupied while I razzle dazzle them," Rebecca replied. "I'll pretend to resist giving it to them for several hours, so don't wait up for me tonight. I should be back by noon tomorrow though," she finished with a wink as she rejoined the Agents, she'd left dangling unaware in suspended animation.

Returning to the doorway where he'd been standing, he smiled thinking to himself, "They don't stand a chance."

After they were moved into the observatory, Rebecca had shared her secret with him, introducing him to the artifact much in the way her mother had introduced it to her dad. After dealing with extraterrestrial communications, crop formations, abduction stories, UFO sightings, and a host of genuine wacko's, the existence of the artifact seemed relatively logical to him, and he couldn't think of anyone more worthy of possessing it.

Taking a seat in her office, he kicked off his shoes and watched the cable news networks' coverage of the launch countdown while waiting for Rebecca's call.

Aboard the US Air Force Learjet, Rebecca made herself comfortable for the ninety-minute flight to DC. She'd traveled the same route in the same or similar aircraft numerous times during almost eight years working on the project. After they got rid of Santa-2012, she was wondering what her next grand endeavor would be as she stared out the window looking down at the snow-covered landscape below.

One thing about the secret service... They were punctual if they were anything, and fifteen minutes later Rebecca was being escorted into a conference room at NASA headquarters where the International Response Task Force representatives and the Director of NASA were already waiting.

"Good afternoon, Director... Ladies and Gentlemen," said Rebecca.

"Professor Doctor Madison!" said the Director. "I'm glad you could fit us in on such short notice."

"It's always a pleasure, Mr. Director," she replied cordially. "How can I be of assistance to you all today?"

"I'll get right to the point," said the Director. "It's come to our attention that key members of the diplomatic task force, feel it would be in the interest of all nations, if every member country possessed their own ignition catalyst for the dark matter containment cells."

Looking around the room, Rebecca asked, "And what interest would that be, other than taking control of *my* proprietary technology, which is no longer needed to activate dark matter energy cells?"

Nervously, the Chinese Ambassador said, "With the United States spearheading the international effort, other countries contributing to the project do not have equal standing without having the original catalyst technology."

"Nor do you require it," stated Rebecca. "Every nation represented here is already using the dark matter containment cells to power most of their energy grids. Activation of the fusion process of further containment cells can be accomplished with any active fusion cell using a simple USB cable, available at any electronics store in the world."

"What if they burn out?" asked the Russian Ambassador.

"Each activated cell has a half-life of a million billion years, Mr. Ambassador," replied Rebecca "and each of those can initiate the fusion process in an unlimited number of future containment cells, so there is not now, nor will there be at any time in the future, the need for my proprietary catalyst technology ever again," she concluded.

The Ambassador from North Korea spoke next, saying "We have provided the project with the world's only device large enough to redirect the incoming projectile from its present path, into the gravitational pull of Jupiter. We have offered that technology in the interest of the entire world. It is only fair that all nations share in the catalyst technology behind the fusion activation process?"

"First of all," replied Rebecca, "The catalyst technology does not belong to the United States. It belongs to me... Professor Doctor Rebecca Madison. No government resources were expended to acquire it, develop it, or harness it, and still my team's technology contributions have ended hunger and poverty in North Korea," she said looking across the room at the North Korean Ambassador. "It's led to a ninety percent decrease in Russia's industrial air pollution levels," she added looking at the Russian diplomat. "In China, we've made it possible to deliver sustainable clean, safe energy to citizens living in even the most remote of villages across your nation," she concluded, looking into the eyes of the Chinese delegate.

"You are all seeking to gain control of something you neither need, nor know how to use, to say nothing of what you'd use it for, if you actually did possess one," said Rebecca looking deliberately into the eyes of everyone seated in the room.

"If this technology is so unneeded," asked the Russian "then why are you so reluctant to share it?"

"Listen," stated Rebecca. "When I was younger, my mother had a recipe for this amazingly delicious, although terribly fattening dessert known as chess pie. Although she never wrote down the recipe, she did teach me how to make it, and showed me the technique she used to ensure it came out perfect every time. Everyone who tasted it, wanted that recipe.

Even though there are dozens of delicious chess pie recipes available on the internet, after tasting my mother's pies, they were never able to replicate the precise flavor or texture and therefore, deemed all of the other recipes inferior."

"The thing is," she continued, "there is no recipe. Either you were there memorizing it as it was created, or you were left with the option of using the great recipes which were readily available from multiple, abundantly available sources."

After a nostalgic pause, Rebecca added "And, you know what? The worst chess pie I've ever had… was still delicious."

"We are not talking about dessert, Professor Doctor Madison," said the North Korean Ambassador. "We are talking about the catalyst for the world's most efficient power source."

"And yet…" stated Rebecca, "They are both exactly the same. Those pies exist in this world because my mother and I exist. Hopefully, she will exist to create chess pies for decades into the future if we all can get back to the business of saving the world."

Continuing, she said "One day when Mom's no longer around, her chess pies will continue to exist through me, and through my children if I should be so blessed. Like those pies, the catalyst exists, because I exist. And while I am more than willing to share them with everyone, the recipe; like the catalyst, lives within me and in that sense, I **am** the catalyst."

Looking around the room, Rebecca could feel the sense of enlightenment seeping into most of the representatives in the room; however, the resolve in the Russian, Chinese, and North Korean delegates was unwavering.

"While I am now craving a pie I previously did not even know exists, for China, I must insist on the recipe for the catalyst," said the Chinese Ambassador.

"As must I for Russia," stated the Russian Ambassador.

"If the other delegates insist, I must also secure the technology for the catalyst, simply to ensure we are all playing on a level playing field," added the North Korean Ambassador.

After stalling for hours while reiterating the absolute absence of a need for the catalyst since the entire world was already using the dark matter containment cells, Rebecca was finally ready to surrender the phony activation code.

Initiating the teleconference with Adam in her office, she used the operating system's remote access portal to retrieve several hundreds of thousands of terabytes of coded nonsense which, due to the alien data compression parameters, would be impossible to open using any operating system other than the one driving the tightly closed local area network operating system in the Boston facility.

Once the near-endless stream of undecipherable code was downloaded onto a twenty-terabyte flash drive, she was ready to prove that both the catalyst program and the passcode actually worked. Connecting the inactive dark matter containment cell with the USB port on the Russian Ambassador's notebook, she asked Adam to input the code, which she projected onto the large plasma viewing screen in the conference room. While everyone was busy copying the information generated digit-by-digit on the viewing screen, Rebecca compressed the time between the appearance of the sixteenth and seventeenth digits of the passcode. Exploiting the perception differential, she used the artifact and USB Charging pad to activate the fusion process inside the containment cell. Afterwards she reconnected the USB cable from the notebook to the now activated dark matter containment cell, placed the charging pad back into her briefcase, and tucked the artifact back beneath her blouse and jacket.

When she exited the time compression bubble, the containment cell seemed to come to life as the final number of the alpha-numeric passcode appeared on the viewing screen. The applause of the task force delegates signaled their approval, as they collected their notes and briefcases and made their way to the exit doors.

Outside the conference as Rebecca was exiting the room, the French Ambassador, unexpectedly grabbed Rebecca's arm as she exited into the hallway, saying "I hope you know; I realize what you've done."

"Really?" replied Rebecca, curiously.

"You have created an interest in your mother's famous dessert which will most assuredly outlast the need for an unnecessary catalyst," stated the Frenchman. "The Russians and Chinese only demanded it in order to claim some form of victory in forcing a compromise with the USA," he added. "Tomorrow, the code will disappear inside the vaults of every member nation present here; however, the recipe for chess pie will live in infamy inside the waistlines of the western world!" Smiling at her, he headed down the empty hallway; his footsteps echoing loudly against the marble floor as he said, "Goodnight Professor Doctor Madison."

"Goodnight, Ambassador," she replied, walking toward Agent Knight, who was waiting with the two additional agents to escort her to her hotel.

During the short ride to the Rosewood Hotel in Washington DC, she checked Google® purely out of curiosity. Chess pie was trending.

CHAPTER 26

Back in Boston, Rebecca and Adam were packing for the trip to Texas, where they would witness the launch at Cape Canaveral, and follow the flight of the three-stage delivery system, first-hand from the Mission Control Center in Houston.

The rest of the world had been holding its collective breath, glued to television screens around the globe as news organizations had been broadcasting the countdown non-stop for almost five years. With fewer than twenty-four hours remaining on the countdown clock, History's longest disaster movie was approaching its grand finale.

If everything went according to plan, the world would be free of this menace which had been hanging over their heads like the sword of Damocles for nearly eight years. Following the seemingly endless approach of the projectile with high-definition images provided courtesy of the Hubble telescope, and blasting them into the homes of billions of people, news organizations had lulled three quarters of the world's population into a state of semi-hypnosis. It was all anyone ever talked about anymore.

Five years earlier, the world watched with high hopes as DSO-Santa-2012 slipped past Saturn's orbit into the more than four-hundred-million-mile void separating it from Jupiter. Based on the number of technological advancements achieved as a result of the research and engineering related to this endeavor, much of the population believed this to be a done deal, and were merely waiting for the culmination of it before lighting their fireworks and popping the corks on their expensive bottles of champagne. Thanks to the energy generated using dark matter energy cells, live images which formerly would have taken an hour to reach Earth were now possible in near-real-time.

The night before the launch, as final inspections were being conducted and checklists annotated, every alarm system in every tracking station in every nation across each continent on the entire planet sounded simultaneously! Rebecca and Adam were touring the Mission Control Center in Houston with the remaining members of the International Response Task Force when the alarm sounded. Upon hearing it, everyone in the group immediately turned their attention to the monitors following the object.

Beneath her sweater, Rebecca could feel the artifact pulsing against her chest. Rushing to the monitoring station she'd been assigned for the mission, she pulled up the telemetry data for the projectile. It was accelerating!

Lights which had been turned off only an hour ago in mission centers across the globe, were turned back on as personnel rushed to their workstations to analyze the new, completely unexpected data pouring in from the network operating system. As it re-calculated the new intercept vectors of the approaching projectile, the launch countdown sequence was updated automatically.

Based on the projectile's increasing velocity and rate of acceleration, the countermeasure would need to be deployed earlier than planned. In fact, they'd lost over four hours!

Fortunately, the majority of the teams had been sequestered within their facilities after the attempted abduction of Professor Doctor Madison and were only minutes away from their workstations. Add to that, the fact that most of them were far too excited to sleep anyway, and a crew of sufficient numbers to execute the required protocols and launch the countermeasure, were in place before the alarms were even silenced.

Both the countermeasure and the backup delivery system had been in place at Cape Canaveral for nearly a week, and the primary vehicle was already fueled and ready for launch. Due to the instantaneous updates made possible by the new operating system, the teams had the updated intercept data at their fingertips almost instantaneously.

Before dawn, the observation area at Playalinda Beach was already filled with people, and once they noticed support vehicles clearing the launch area much earlier than expected, the word spread quickly that something had changed. Soon afterwards, reports started pouring in from independent observatories and news agencies around the world as the launch team hustled to meet the accelerated launch time.

It was an exceedingly small deployment window calculated by the operating system, which had to account for the differences in planetary positions as well as the increasing velocity of the incoming projectile. Amazingly, the launch team was ready nearly seventy minutes before the accelerated launch time.

Hoping the additional time could work to their advantage, Rebecca calculated the effect of allowing the warhead to reach the incoming projectile sooner. The operating system immediately showed an eight percent increase in the warhead's probability of shoving it into Jupiter's gravitational field. Still, that success estimate was thirty percent lower than those calculated for the original intercept plan.

"Okay team!" said Rebecca. "We are ready for launch right now, and every two minutes we wait lowers our chance of success by another one percent."

Across the room, the Director shouted, "Start the countdown."

"No!" countered Professor Doctor Madison. "Launch the damn rocket!"

Quickly acknowledging the need for immediate action, the Director shouted, "You heard the woman! Launch that goddamned thing... Now!"

Briefly nodding at the Director in appreciation, she said "Thank you Mr. Director. I apologize for the outburst."

The reaction over at Playalinda Beach was startling for onlookers. They were accustomed to following the ten-minute countdown clock, and news reporters were caught off guard as the gondola's massive engines came to life, propelling the vehicle quickly into the grey morning sky over Cape Canaveral.

Inside the Mission Control Center, and in locations around the globe, everyone watched in nervous anticipation as the gondola pushed the outer atmospheric delivery system high into the air at a velocity never witnessed before. Within minutes it had reached terminal velocity, jettisoning the dark matter propulsion system upward into the Earth's magnetosphere. As it reached the cusp and the magnetic field generator came online, the vehicle instantly vanished! Seconds later, the familiar blue glow of the dark matter reaction chambers came to life, visibly pushing it toward the rendezvous point at the speed of light.

The vehicle's velocity increased steadily as it raced through the darkness of space toward Jupiter. Thirty minutes into the operation, the instantaneous updates provided by the operating system sounded the alarms again. The velocity of the approaching projectile had also increased.

Based on the new telemetry, it would reach the rendezvous point four minutes too early for the warhead to successfully redirect it into Jupiter's gravitational field. Suddenly, it looked as if the North Korean option would be the only viable one remaining.

Inside the Mission Control Center, the delegates from the International Response Task Force were huddled together around the Director when Rebecca approached them.

"We need to adjust the trajectory," stated the Director. "Our weapon will reach the object too late, and letting that thing continue unabated towards Earth is not an option."

"Yes, I know," Replied Rebecca. "I also realize North Korea has great confidence in their warhead, but I still suggest we begin fueling the second gondola... Just in case."

"What good will that do, Professor Doctor Madison? We don't have another warhead large enough to confront that thing, and at its current velocity it will reach Earth in only a matter of months!"

"I understand," replied Rebecca, "But please, begin fueling up the second gondola, and get me back to Boston as soon as possible. If the nuke doesn't stop that thing, we're going to need a back-up plan and everything I need to work out that plan is in my office back in Boston."

Looking around the room, the Director saw that everyone was listening and waiting for his decision. "Okay," he said. "Fuel up the second gondola and get Professor Doctor Madison back to Boston ASAP!"

Agent Knight and the escort team rushed to the helicopter pad outside Mission Control with Rebecca and Adam. Fewer than ten minutes later, they were aboard the Learjet headed down the taxiway and were immediately cleared for take-off. As they viewed the mission from the live feed on the aircraft, they watched intently as the dark matter propulsion system released the two-hundred-megaton payload and fired its retro boosters.

The whole world stared transfixed as surveillance satellites tracked the two objects rapidly approaching one another. Inside the Mission Control Center, the pompous North Korean ambassador was almost giddy as the retinal filters on the satellite cameras activated seconds before the moment of truth.

Viewing the impact, even through the darkened lenses of a satellite camera monitoring the event from millions of miles away, the flash of the thermonuclear detonation was blinding. While tracking devices were able to confirm a direct hit, it took several seconds for the auto-focus on the satellite cameras to modulate their light filter frequencies enough to peer into the glowing blast zone.

As the images slowly came back into focus, the projectile's velocity had been cut in half and the surface was glowing white hot after absorbing the energy dispersed by the blast. Otherwise, it was completely undamaged and still in one piece.

In the literal blink of an eye, the celebratory air with which the day had begun, devolved into immobilizing terror as Earth's population realized, the incoming projectile had taken our planet's most lethal punch and shrugged it off as if it were nothing.

Once on the ground in Boston, Adam and Rebecca were met on the tarmac by a driver who swiftly transported them and Agent Knight back to the Observatory. Once inside the compound, Rebecca and Adam ran into her office, where she opened the safe concealed in the floor beneath her desk and removed a silver briefcase. After a quick peek inside to make sure the contents were indeed there and intact, the two of them left the office immediately, rushing back outside to the car still idling in the parking lot.

Once inside the vehicle, she said "We need to get to Cape Canaveral right away!"

With that, the driver sped back down the access road with the skill of a Formula One racecar pilot. In minutes, they were re-boarding the Learjet and cleared for takeoff, headed for Florida with clearance to land directly on the airstrip at Cape Canaveral.

When the plane came to a stop and the stairs were lowered, a driver was already waiting to transport them directly to the launch tower where the second gondola was fueled and ready for launch. The driver dropped them off at the base of the tower, where they entered the elevator waiting to carry them all the way up to the cone of the dud warhead.

During the construction of the mock device, Rebecca had instructed the engineering team to include a special compartment inside the titanium nose cone, built to her exacting specifications. Furthermore, the compartment was to remain locked, with her possessing the only key which would open it. Other than Rebecca, only Adam and Professor Doctor Stephan Wagner knew about the compartment, which had remained unopened and unused up until now. The seams of the opening were so precisely manufactured, that they were virtually undetectable.

At the Mission Control Center in Houston, the Director of NASA had been monitoring Professor Doctor Madison since she entered the elevator. All aspects of the tower were under seamless observation by hundreds of cameras installed at various points inside the structure.

Reaching inside the briefcase, Rebecca first removed the key, using it to open the compartment door. Next, she removed what appeared to be a modified dark matter containment cell, outfitted with an additional compartment above the fusion chamber containing the active dark matter.

Using the same key which opened the compartment in the nose cone, she unlocked the compartment atop the fusion chamber and opened it. Next, she lifted the deerskin pouch from around her neck and opened it, dumping the artifact into the palm of her hand. Carefully, she placed it inside the small chamber at the top of the active containment cell.

Even after eight years of working with and around her every single day, aside from Adam, no one had ever noticed the pouch around her neck, or seen the object she'd removed from it. While they could clearly observe her actions from the Mission Control Center, they were unable to communicate with her to ask what she was doing. Nevertheless, no one would have dreamt of interfering as they watched her prepare the modified cell.

Once the artifact was in place, she locked the compartment door of the containment cell and placed it inside the hidden chamber of the nose cone where it snapped securely into place. Using the same key, she pre-set the spring-loaded locks on the inside of the compartment door, then inserted it into another keyhole inside the nose cone. Rotating it one quarter turn to the right, it clicked into place, unlocking the plunger mechanism positioned directly over the top of the artifact and modified dark matter containment cell. She left the key in place when she closed the compartment door, deploying the internal locks and making it impossible to re-open from the outside.

With the empty case in hand, they returned to the elevator and descended to the base of the tower, where the driver was waiting to take them back to the Learjet. Fifteen minutes later, they were wheels up, and on the way back to the Mission Control Center in Houston.

CHAPTER 27

Upon entering the Mission Control Center, Rebecca was besieged by questions fired at her from the NASA Director and members of the task force delegation. "Exactly what did you install in that warhead?" asked the Director.

"It was the same active dark matter found in every other containment cell," replied Rebecca.

"And the object you put inside the chamber at the top?"

"That, Sir... was a gift given to me by my mother over ten years ago."

"That, Professor Doctor Madison, is the property of the United States Government!" shouted the Director, pointing to two side-by-side images displayed on the monitor screens. "The object you placed in the containment cell, was in government custody and has a fucking Department of Defense catalog number assigned to it!"

"Correction," said Professor Doctor Madison. "That object was being detained by the Department of Defense, but it never... ever... belonged to them."

"Who are you to..." started the Director, before being cut off in mid-sentence by Rebecca.

"Listen, Mr. Director," said Rebecca. "We can either stand here debating who owns what, or we can do something about that missile out their headed right at us! Unless we destroy that thing before it gets past the asteroid belt, all the debate in the world will be pointless, because everyone on this planet will be dead!"

Having had access to the video feeds which captured Rebecca installing the alien device into the nose cone, the

Chinese and Russian ambassadors demanded an explanation. North Korea was already claiming their warhead had been sabotaged, and that it was obviously a plot by NASA and the Department of Defense to undermine North Korea's standing among other nuclear nations.

As the various random chatter built to a crescendo inside the Mission Control Center, the telemetry alarm sounded again, snatching everyone in the building back into the moment. The massive projectile was accelerating again!

One of the mission control specialists said, "Sir, what are your orders? We need to do something, because that thing out there is back on course for Earth, and now it's hot enough to vaporize our atmosphere before it even reaches the surface!"

"How is that even possible?" asked the Director. "The temperature out there is near absolute zero. It should be cooling off almost instantly!"

"What it **should** do, and what it **is** doing, are two entirely different things," replied the mission control specialist. "According to our sensors, it has absorbed and retained every bit of the heat produced by the nuclear blast, and its surface temperature is now hotter than the sun!"

"Sir," stated Rebecca. "We need to launch the gondola right now. If that object out there makes it past the asteroid belt and reaches Mars, we won't need to take it out anymore, because it will roast the planet before it even reaches us."

"Aw, fuck it!" sighed the Director. "Launch the goddamned thing... and if mankind survives this, Professor Doctor Madison, you and I are going to have a serious conversation regarding NASA protocols."

"I seriously doubt that," said Rebecca, as the gondola engines ignited, lifting the Deep Space Delivery System into the clear afternoon skies over Florida.

With the lighter nose cone, the gondola accelerated much faster, delivering stage two of the transport system to the cusp of the magnetic field where it activated and disappeared out of sight until the blue glow of the dark matter fusion drive appeared. Once it did, NASA lost complete control of the delivery vehicle.

As the alarm system sounded yet again, it was accompanied by the flashing display across all the monitors inside the Mission Control Center... GUIDANCE SYSTEM DISENGAGED.

"What the Hell?!" shouted the Director. "Who's controlling this damn thing?"

"It's the artifact, Sir," said Rebecca. "It's going home."

As everyone in the Mission Control Center turned to watch the delivery system and the incoming projectile streaking towards each other, the telemetry data coming into the monitoring stations was staggering. Both objects were moving at nearly twice the speed of light.

Once the incoming projectile exited the invisible dark matter surrounding Jupiter's magnetic field, the velocity of the delivery system tripled, activating the automated lens retinas of the observation satellites only a micro-second before the two opposing objects collided.

Looking around the Mission Control Center, Adam noticed that everything had stopped. To his left, he noticed Rebecca was smiling up at him. Smiling back at her, they turned to face each other.

She extended her forearms to him with her palms up, and he placed his on top of them, palms down. As they had done many times before, they pressed their foreheads together and closed their eyes. Without words, she spoke to him.

"We're about to go back, My Love," she said. "Back to before the blue lights, and monster planetoids, and mystery catalysts, and all of... this."

Adam smiled as he listened, but he didn't interrupt.

Rebecca continued, saying "We will still meet, and I will still love you, and our lives will go on, but you know as well as I do that mankind is not yet ready to wield this technology. Even as the world was coming to an end, we couldn't unify as a society, and put our personal differences aside for humanity's sake."

"The planetoid was never the test," Rebecca said. "It was always us. How we treat each other, and show compassion for one another, and pull each other up instead of tearing one another down for the sake of power; that was the real test. While we may have figured out how to solve one big problem, it's the little ones we have yet to master, that are preventing us from joining the rest of the intergalactic community."

Adam nodded in understanding, as they opened their eyes to look at one another.

"I will find you," said Adam. "Nothing on Earth *or* in the stars will ever keep me from you."

"I know that," said Rebecca leaning in and kissing him. After the kiss, she asked "Are you ready for this? It's going to be spectacular!"

Nodding, Adam held her hand as they turned to face the enormous monitor screen bathing the team inside the Mission Control Center in an eerie blue light. Slowly, Rebecca released her grip on time while she and Adam watched in ultra-slow motion, as the flash generated by the dark matter warhead completely engulfed the incoming planetoid.

Both the delivery vehicle and the projectile were instantly vaporized in the resulting detonation which could clearly be seen from Earth, even against the brightness of the mid-afternoon sky.

Simultaneously, all of the dark matter containment cells in our solar system; the fusion of which had been activated by the original catalyst, flared, creating a flash which could be observed even from distant galaxies billions of light years from Earth.

"It is with great pleasure that we present this year's Nobel Prize for Physics to Doctor Rebecca Jocelyn Madison!"

As thunderous applause filled the ballroom of the convention center in Oslo, Norway, everyone was on their feet as Rebecca stood and walked gracefully toward the stage to accept the award. When she approached the table where Adam Levinson was standing, she stopped and turned to him, saying "You are a beautiful, beautiful man," before tiptoeing and kissing him quickly on the lips.

As the applause and laughter intensified following the unexpected detour, she stepped back adding "Don't wait ten years to find me, okay?"

Adam watched with a smile as this breathtaking genius turned and continued to the stage wearing what he thought was the most mesmerizing black cocktail dress he had ever seen.

CHAPTER 28

"And what shall we make of the Earth experiment?" asked Zyrtu.

"Our data is inconclusive," replied Baltor. "The actions of the dominant species are puzzling, as they seem to be counterintuitive and at odds with their own best interests."

"Agreed," responded Zyrtu. "However, they have succeeded in reaching their pre-determined evolutionary milestone. We are obliged to allow their continued evolution as the dominant species."

"I concur," said Baltor. "However, even we cannot prevent them from destroying themselves. They are a petulant, unruly species who view every technological advancement through the lens of war. Their downfall will not come as a result of extraterrestrial interference, but rather from their own internal proliferation of intolerance, and their unwillingness to choose cooperation over conflict."

"And your edict, Baltor... What say you?" asked Zyrtu.

"Were all of the fusion chambers removed by the flash during the reset?" asked Baltor.

"They were," replied Zyrtu.

"Then they shall remain in isolation for the next cycle, having no access to knowledge or technology from other, more advanced civilizations within the extended human genetic omniverse," Baltor pronounced. "Furthermore, all encounters with them shall be suspended immediately, and all test subjects returned to Earth Prime, including those currently detained for scientific study and evaluation. Pending completion of their evolutionary evaluation at the conclusion of the next cycle, they shall be left... alone."

"Your edict is duly recorded, and the new cycle has been initiated," replied Zyrtu.

As they returned to the bridge of their exploratory vessel, Baltor said, "They are a flawed, yet wonderful civilization, Zyrtu. Even in their haste to destroy their own planet, they are able to create wonderful, amazing things using only the simplest of elements."

"These things of which you speak; what might they be?" asked Zyrtu.

"Using the infertile ovum of domesticated poultry and two simple derivatives of the lactose-based nutrient produced by maternal bovine surrogates, they combine those things with crushed triticum, the acidic residue of fermented malus, and crystalized sucrose inside a circular containment vessel before subjecting it to low level thermal radiation inside a rudimentary containment chamber," Baltor explained. "The resulting delicacy is known as 'Chess Pie'."

Scanning the database on his communication module, Zyrtu said "Yes, it is cataloged in Earth's nutritional database. I can replicate it for you if you wish."

"No," replied Baltor, nostalgically. "The result differs substantially when produced by nutritional replicators and is inferior to those of the educator... Jocelyn Madison."

THE END.

RIANO D. MCFARLAND – Author Information

Riano McFarland is an American author and professional entertainer from Las Vegas, Nevada, with an international history.

Born in Germany in 1963, he is both the son of a Retired US Air Force Veteran and an Air Force Veteran himself. After spending 17 years in Europe and achieving notoriety as an international recording artist, he moved to Las Vegas, Nevada in 1999, where he quickly established himself as a successful entertainer. Having literally thousands of successful performances under his belt, *Riano* is a natural when it comes to dealing with and communicating his message to audiences. His sincere smile and easygoing nature quickly put acquaintances at ease with him, allowing him to connect with them on a much deeper personal level—something which contributes substantially to his emotionally riveting style of storytelling. Furthermore, having lived in or visited many of the areas described in his novels, he can connect the readers to those places using factual descriptions and impressions, having personally observed them.

Riano has been writing poetry, essays, short stories, tradeshow editorials, and talent information descriptions for over 40 years, collectively. His style stands apart from many authors in that, while his talent for weaving clues into the very fabric of his stories gives them depth and a sense of credulity, each of his novels are distinctly different from one another. Whether describing the relationship between a loyal dog and his loving owner in **ODIN**, following the development of an introverted boy-genius in **JAKE'S DRAGON**, exploring the parallels between people and the objects they hold sacred in **I FIX BROKEN THINGS**, or describing an alternative world view as observed by a dog in **THE WORLD ACCORDING TO BANDIT**, *Riano* tactfully draws you into an inescapable web of emotional involvement with each additional chapter and each new character introduced. Added to that, his painstaking research when developing plots and storylines gives his novels substance which can hold up under even the staunchest of reader scrutiny.

Possessing an uncanny flair for building creative tension and suspense within a realistic plot, *Riano* pulls readers into the story as if they were, themselves, always intended to have a starring role in it. Furthermore, by skillfully blending historical fact with elements of fiction *Riano* makes the impossible appear plausible, while his intensely detailed descriptions bring characters and locations vividly into focus.

   Although it's certain you'll love the destination to which he'll deliver you, you'll never guess the routes he'll take to get you there, so you may as well just dive in and enjoy the ride which is certain to keep you on the edge of your seat until the very last paragraph!

Made in the USA
San Bernardino, CA
21 May 2020